Praise for Marta Perry

"Set within the Amish community, with a strong, sympathetic heroine at the center of a suspenseful plot, Perry's story hooks you immediately."
—*RT Book Reviews* on *Home by Dark*

"Perry's strong writing, along with loads of suspense, will keep you turning the pages."
—*RT Book Reviews* on *Danger in Plain Sight*

Praise for Diane Burke

"A fascinating story of hidden identities and forbidden love, creating a page-turning mystery."
—*RT Book Reviews* on *Double Identity*

"Burke's solid mystery has characters who are easy to empathize with."
—*RT Book Reviews* on *Midnight Caller*

Praise for Kit Wilkinson

"This excellent story builds an intriguing mystery around a developing romance in the fascinating world of competitive steeplechase."
—*RT Book Reviews* on *Sabotage*

"Plenty of action, a heartwarming love story and a good mystery make this a compelling read."
—*RT Book Reviews* on *Protector's Honor*

MARTA PERRY

A lifetime spent in rural Pennsylvania, where she still lives, and her own Pennsylvania Dutch roots led Marta Perry to write about the Plain People and their rich heritage in her current fiction series for Berkley Books and Harlequin HQN. Marta recently celebrated the publication of her fifty-first novel, with another eight books scheduled to be released over the next two years. The two-time RITA® Award finalist has more than six million copies of her books in print.

Marta is a member of RWA, ACFW, Novelists, Inc., and Pennwriters. When she's not writing, she and her husband enjoy traveling, gardening and spending time with their six beautiful grandchildren.

DIANE BURKE,

an award-winning author, took first place in the inspirational category for a Daphne du Maurier Award for Excellence in Mystery and Suspense and has been a finalist for an ACFW Carol Award and a Laurel Wreath.

Diane lives on the east coast of Florida and, because of the glorious weather, beach and surf, feels as if she is on a permanent vacation. She has three sons, five grandchildren and three stepgrandchildren, who keep her on her toes and fill her life with love.

Her author page is www.amazon.com/author/diane-burke. She loves to hear from her readers and can be reached at diane@dianeburkeauthor.com.

KIT WILKINSON

is a former Ph.D. student who once wrote discussions on the medieval feminine voice. She now prefers weaving stories of romance and redemption. Her first inspirational manuscript won a prestigious RWA Golden Heart Award and her second has been nominated for an RT Reviewers' Choice Award. You can visit with Kit at www.kitwilkinson.com or write to her at write@kitwilkinson.com.

DANGER IN AMISH COUNTRY

MARTA PERRY
DIANE BURKE
KIT WILKINSON

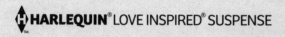

HARLEQUIN® LOVE INSPIRED® SUSPENSE

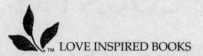 LOVE INSPIRED BOOKS

Recycling programs for this product may not exist in your area.

ISBN-13: 978-0-373-67577-7

DANGER IN AMISH COUNTRY

Copyright © 2013 by Harlequin Books S.A.

The publisher acknowledges the copyright holders of the individual works as follows:

FALL FROM GRACE
Copyright © 2013 by Martha Johnson

DANGEROUS HOMECOMING
Copyright © 2013 by Diane Burke

RETURN TO WILLOW TRACE
Copyright © 2013 by Kit Wilkinson

CONTENTS

FALL FROM GRACE

MARTA PERRY

This story is dedicated to my husband, as always.

But they who wait for the Lord shall renew their strength; they shall mount up with wings like eagles; they shall run and not be weary; they shall walk and not faint.
—*Isaiah* 40:31

ONE

Sara Esch smiled as her young scholars burst out into the autumn sunshine at the end of another school day. Even the best of Amish students couldn't help showing a bit of enthusiasm when freedom arrived at three o'clock each weekday afternoon, especially on Friday.

All except one, it seemed. Seven-year-old Rachel King hung back, her small face solemn, as if reluctant to leave her desk.

Sara tried not to let concern show in her expression as she approached the motherless child. Rachel had been in Sara's one-room school for less than a month, since she and her father arrived in Beaver Creek, coming to Pennsylvania from Indiana. That meant Sara didn't know Rachel as well as she did most of the *kinner* in her school.

Sara knelt next to the child and spoke softly, knowing her words would be masked by the chatter of the two eighth-grade girls whose turn it was to wash the chalkboards.

"*Was ist letz,* Rachel?" She asked the question in dialect. She always spoke Englisch in school, but the familiar tongue of home and family might put the child at ease. "What's wrong?"

"Nothing." Rachel's round blue eyes grew rounder still, as if she was surprised that her teacher had noticed. "Nothing is wrong, Teacher Sara."

Sara sat back on her heels, studying the small face. Rachel might have been any young Amish girl, with her blue eyes, rosy cheeks, and blond hair. Her plain blue dress and black apron were like those of every other little girl, too. But something was different about Rachel King, of that Sara was certain sure.

She took the child's hands in hers. "You can tell me if anything is troubling you, Rachel. I want you to be happy here in Beaver Creek."

Rachel's lips trembled, as if she were on the verge of speech. Then she looked over Sara's shoulder, and her expression lightened.

"Daed!" She ran to the man who filled the schoolhouse doorway.

So. Sara got slowly to her feet, mindful of Caleb King's gaze on her. His arrival meant she wouldn't hear anything more from Rachel today. But at least she could see that Rachel's problem, whatever it was, wasn't with her father. She would hate to have to deal with such an issue.

She took a step toward Caleb, smiling, and stopped when she encountered an icy glare. His face was set in severe lines above the warm chestnut of his beard, and Caleb's gaze seemed an accusation. Her heart gave an uncomfortable thump.

Caleb patted his daughter's head. "Go out and play on the swings. I need to talk to Teacher Sara."

Sara caught a swift flare of panic in the child's face at the prospect of going outside. She moved toward them.

"Perhaps Rachel could help with washing the boards," she suggested. "We might step out onto the porch to talk."

Caleb's gray-blue eyes grew steely with annoyance, probably at her interference, but he nodded. He stepped back and held the door open like a command.

Sara pushed Rachel gently toward the chalkboard. "Lily and Lovina, you'll like to have Rachel help you for a bit, ain't so?"

Lily looked a tad mulish at the prospect, but gentle Lovina seemed to take the situation in and smiled, holding out her hand to the child.

"*Ya, komm,* Rachel."

The little girl ran toward her happily enough. Satisfied, Sara stepped through the door, very aware of Caleb's looming presence behind her. He had a complaint, it seemed.

The door clicked shut.

"What has happened at school to bring my child home so upset she could not even eat her supper?" Caleb didn't give Sara time to turn around before he threw the words at her. "And to give her nightmares, as well? I don't expect this at an Amish school."

Stiffening at the implication she was at fault, Sara made an effort to keep her expression calm as she faced the man. "I noticed that Rachel seemed upset today. I was just trying to get her to tell me what was wrong when you came in."

And whatever it is, I am not to blame, she added silently. Nothing was more important to her than her scholars—they were the only *kinner* she was ever likely to have.

"You didn't scold her for anything yesterday?" Caleb didn't look mollified. "Or let another child bully her?"

"Certainly not. Bullying is not tolerated in my classroom." She took a deep breath, reminding herself not to let the man's antagonism rouse her temper. Even teachers in Amish schools had to learn to deal with troublesome parents. "I am as puzzled as you are. Maybe together we can figure out how to handle this problem."

She met his gaze steadily, and after what seemed a very long moment, she had the satisfaction of seeing some of his antagonism fade.

"Sorry. I didn't mean… *Ach,* I was worried."

Caleb seemed to realize belatedly that he still wore his black hat. He took it off, revealing hair the same chestnut as his beard. His face was lean and austere close-up, and there were fine lines around his cool eyes. He was a widower, so the rumors ran, his wife having died after a long illness. It was natural that he'd be protective of his only child. But not natural at all that he should immediately assume she was at fault.

Sara gathered her scattered wits to concentrate on the problem at hand. "I thought Rachel seemed a little reluctant to leave school yesterday. That's why I made sure the Miller children walked along with her. She didn't give you any idea of what was troubling her?"

Caleb shook his head, worry deepening the lines in his face. "When I heard her crying in the night, she sounded so afraid. The only thing she said made no sense. She said Der Alte would get her."

"The Old Man?" Relief swept through Sara. "So that's it."

"What's it?" Caleb demanded, his fists clenching. "Who is this old man who frightened my child?"

"*Ach,* it's not real." She put her hand on his arm in an automatic gesture of reassurance and felt taut muscle beneath the fabric of his coat. She pulled her hand away as if she'd touched something hot, realizing she was probably blushing. She'd treated him as she would one of her three brothers, but he was a stranger, despite being Amish.

"*Komm.*" She moved quickly off the schoolhouse porch, just as glad to turn her back on him. "I'll show you."

The schoolhouse sat in the fertile Beaver Creek Valley. Amish farms stretched out on either side, while in front of the schoolhouse the long lane led to the paved county road that entered the town of Beaver Creek a bit over a mile east.

Sara turned away from the road, heading across the

playground behind the school. Here the ground sloped down to the creek for which the valley was named.

On the other side of the creek the wooded ridge went sharply upward, seeming to lean over the valley protectively. No year-round houses had been built there, but the ridge was dotted with hunting cabins that would be busy during deer season.

"Where are you going?" Caleb's long strides kept up with hers. "Are you going to answer me about this old man? Does he live back here?"

"In a way." She raised her arm to point. "See that rocky outcropping? Watch what happens when we move just a little farther."

A few steps took them to the spot where the rocky cliff suddenly took on a different aspect, its sharp edges forming what a child's imagination might see as the profile of an old man.

A quick glance at Caleb's face showed that he understood. "Der Alte," she said. "The *kinner* call it that. I forgot that you wouldn't know."

Caleb stared at the rocky profile, frowning. "*Ya,* I see. But I don't understand what there is about it to frighten her so."

"Nor I." Her voice firmed. "But I mean to find out. If one of the older scholars has been telling scary stories to the young ones, that is not—" She broke off, her gaze arrested by something dark at the base of the cliff face. "Look there. That…that almost looks like—"

"A person." Caleb finished for her. "Someone is lying there."

* * *

Caleb's thoughts fled to Rachel. But his little girl was safe enough in the schoolroom, and if someone was lying hurt across the creek, he must go help.

"Go back to the *kinner*," he said shortly. "I'll see what's happened." He didn't take more than a few steps before realizing that Teacher Sara was right behind him. He swung around, exasperated. "I said—"

"If someone is hurt, it's better we both go. Then one can stay with the injured person while the other runs for help."

A look at her stubborn face told him arguing would do no good. Heaven preserve him from a headstrong woman. Not wasting his breath, he ran toward the creek.

"This way," she said, panting a little. "Stepping-stones."

He nodded and veered after her as she headed downstream. No doubt the teacher knew the area better than he did. If the man was injured badly enough to need a stretcher, she'd know the best way for emergency workers to get to him, as well as the closest telephone.

And if it was worse? He didn't have a clear line of sight now, but that dark form had been ominously still. Well, he'd tried to protect Teacher Sara from going. If she saw something bad, it was her own fault.

She was already starting across the stream, jumping lightly from one flat stone to another. He followed, but when they reached the other side, he took the lead again, brushing through the undergrowth toward the base of the cliff.

They broke through into the pebbly scree at the bottom of the cliff. Any hope he'd had that the form was an animal or fallen log vanished.

Sara reached the man first. She dropped to her knees, her skirt pooling around her, and put her fingers on his neck. Caleb could tell her that she wouldn't find a pulse. No one could still be alive when his head looked like that. The poor man didn't have a chance.

Moving quickly to her, Caleb took Sara's arm. *"Komm,"* he said, his voice gruff. "There's nothing you can do."

He helped her up, eyeing her face. If she was going to faint on him… But though her normally pink cheeks were dead white, Teacher Sara seemed to have herself in hand.

"Poor man," she murmured, and he thought she was praying silently, as he was.

"Do you know him?" He drew her back a step or two, keeping his hand on her elbow in case she was unsteady on her feet.

Sara shook her head. "Englisch," she said unnecessarily. If the man had been Amish, she'd certainly have known him. "He looks fairly young." Her tone was pitying.

Young, *ya.* The fellow wore jeans and boots, like so many young Englischers. Dark hair, with a stubble of beard on his chin. He looked… Caleb sought for the right word. He looked tough. That was it. Like some-one you might not want to get on the wrong side of.

But they couldn't stand here wondering about him. "It doesn't seem right to leave the poor man alone. If I stay with him, can you see to calling the police?" Amish usually tried to steer clear of entanglement with the law, but their duty was clear in this case.

"Ya." Sara took a step back, away from the support of his hand. "There's an Englisch house not far. They'll have a phone. And then I'll stay with the *kinner*."

"My Rachel." His gaze met Sara's. "You don't think she could have seen this?" He gestured toward the body, his mind rebelling at the thought of his little girl viewing anything so gruesome.

"No." Sara seemed to push the idea away with both hands. "I don't think... Surely he hasn't been lying there since yesterday."

"It's possible." He looked up at the cliff face above them. From this angle it just looked like a jumble of rocks. "If she was standing where we stood..." He stopped, looking at Teacher Sara accusingly. "You shouldn't let the *kinner* go so far from the school."

"It is the edge of the playground," she said, a touch of anger like lightning in her green eyes. "The schol-ars are never out of my sight when they have recess."

"Sorry," he muttered.

He shouldn't blame Teacher Sara, when the thing that troubled him was his own inability to get his child to confide in him. Rachel had been so distant and solemn since her mother's death, as if all Rachel's laughter had been buried with Barbara.

"I'll go now," Teacher Sara said, turning away stiffly.

He let his gaze linger on her slender figure until the undergrowth hid her from sight. No matter how long this took, he knew instinctively that she would stay with Rachel. She'd attempt to comfort his little girl.

But if Rachel really had seen this man lying dead… His thoughts stuttered to a halt as something even worse occurred to him. What if his little girl had seen the man fall?

TWO

"I'm not sure what else we can tell you, Chief O'Brian." Sara tried not to think how odd it was to see the bulky, gray-haired township police chief sitting behind the teacher's desk in the Amish schoolhouse. "Neither of us knows who the man was."

She and Caleb were perched atop the first graders' desks, which were, of course, the row closest to her desk. It was not exactly comfortable, but she kept her hands folded in her lap and her feet, in their sedate black shoes, together on the wide planks of the wooden floor.

Chief O'Brian, benevolent and grandfatherly, had guided the small police presence that covered both the village of Beaver Creek and the rural township since before Sara was born. He consulted the notes he'd been making and then looked up at her.

A girlish giggle floated in from the porch, distracting him. Lily and Lovina were teaching Rachel how to play jacks under the observant gaze of a young officer. Sara felt sure that the giggle, coming from Lily, was for the benefit of the policeman.

She'd chide the girl, but she was too relieved that

they were well screened from the efforts under way across the creek, where the emergency crew was removing the body.

"Well, now." Chief O'Brian returned to the subject at hand. "I think there's just one thing that's not quite clear to me, Teacher Sara. Why exactly were you and Mr. King out there looking at the ridge to begin with?"

She opened her mouth to answer, but Caleb beat her to it.

"My little girl was telling me something I couldn't make heads or tails of about an old man," he said. "When I picked her up after school today, I asked Teacher Sara about it. She showed me the way the rock outcropping looks like a face in profile."

"Caleb and his daughter are new to Beaver Creek," Sara said, although she suspected that the police chief, like the Amish bishop, knew all there was to know about newcomers. "You know how the *kinner* talk about that face they think they see in the rocks." She turned to Caleb. "Chief O'Brian visits our school several times a year. He teaches the scholars how to be safe when they're walking along the roads. And brings them candy canes at Christmas, ain't so?"

Chief O'Brian's lined face relaxed in a smile. "Visiting the schools is my favorite part of my job. Not like this situation." He jerked his thumb in the direction of the ridge.

Caleb's explanation had made it sound as if Rachel's questions about the old man were mere curiosity. No doubt he was relieved that the chief had moved away from the topic.

"I'm sorry for the man's family to be getting news like this," she said. "Do you know who he was?"

"Not yet," Chief O'Brian said. "So you folks were just looking over that way out of idle curiosity, is that it?"

Apparently he wasn't ready to move away from the topic after all. Sara glanced at the poster above the chalkboard, which proclaimed *Visitors are the sunshine in our day* in cursive letters.

She could practically feel the intensity of Caleb's will directed toward her. For whatever reason, he didn't want her to say anything more about Rachel.

"I…I suppose so." Sara tried to sound confident, but it went against her nature even to imply something that wasn't true. She could feel her cheeks growing warm.

"I see." Chief O'Brian looked from her to Caleb, and her flush deepened. Now he was thinking exactly the wrong thing, supposing she'd made an excuse to walk with Caleb. But to say anything more would just make things worse.

Fortunately, Chief O'Brian was distracted by a gesture from the officer on the porch. He rose, very authoritative in his gray uniform.

"Well, I guess I won't be bothering you good folks any longer. Mr. King, I'm sure you want to be getting your little girl home. Sara, sorry for the disruption."

Sara murmured something, she wasn't sure what, just glad for the moment to see him leaving her classroom. He paused for a second on the porch to say something that made the girls giggle again, and then he and the young officer headed off toward the police car.

Sara swung to face Caleb. "Why didn't you tell Chief O'Brian the truth about Rachel?"

Caleb's strong-featured face tightened. "I didn't lie to the man."

"You told him only part of the truth," she snapped, keeping her voice low so that the children on the porch couldn't hear. "And you involved me in saying less than the truth, as well."

Caleb had a remarkably stubborn jaw. "My child's nightmares are not his business."

"It might be important that Rachel was so upset last night about the Old Man. It might mean…" Sara let that thought trickle to a stop, afraid of where it was going.

"Ya." His face was bleak. "It might mean that my Rachel saw something bad. And if so, it's for me to deal with. Not you. And I'm certain sure not the police."

He stalked out of the schoolhouse, leaving Sara with nothing at all to say.

The gentle clink of plates accompanied the evening routine of helping her *mamm* with the dishes. Sara, her hands in the warm, soapy water, found the chore comforting after the stresses of the day.

"I can finish up, Mamm, if you want." Her mother looked a bit tired, but she wouldn't want to hear Sara say so.

"No need." Her mother polished a plate with her usual vigor. "I don't mind. I remember when you girls used to make so much noise with washing dishes I had to get away."

Sara smiled. True enough. When she and Trudy and Ruthie did the dishes, they'd chattered and laughed and argued the whole time. But now Trudy and Ruthie were married, as well as her two oldest brothers, and Trudy had twins on the way.

Funny. Sara, the oldest, had been the first one to plan a wedding, but Tommy Brand had managed to postpone it for one reason or another for nearly five years. And when he did get married, it was to someone else.

"I'm wonderful glad Caleb King was with you when you saw that poor man." Mamm set a bowl on the shelf. "I wouldn't like to think of you finding him all alone."

Mamm didn't like to think of her doing anything alone. She was still trying to marry off her maidal daughter.

"*Ya,* I'm glad he was there, too." Sara kept her tone neutral. "Lily and Lovina had stayed after school to help, so they were there to watch his little girl."

"They're *gut* girls, even if that Lily is a bit flighty," Mamm said. "So, Caleb is a fine-looking man, ain't so? And I hear Josiah King is wonderful glad to have his nephew there to help out while he's laid up. Maybe Caleb will even decide to stay, *ya?*"

"Stop matchmaking," Sara said with mock severity. "I'm not looking for a husband."

"*Ya,* but they're nice to have, all the same." Her mother's eyes twinkled.

"And then who'd be here to help with the dishes?" Sara retorted, smiling. "If I—" She stopped at the sound of voices in the living room, where Daed had been settled in his favorite chair, reading *The Budget,* the Amish newspaper.

She exchanged glances with her mother. "That sounds like Chief O'Brian."

"You'll be wanted, then, ain't so?" Mamm handed her a towel. "Dry your hands and hurry in."

Sara touched her hair to be sure it went smoothly under her white organdy *kapp* and shook out the apron that matched her green dress. She reached the living room just as her *daed* called out for her.

"Chief O'Brian is here to talk about that poor man you found." Daed pushed his glasses up on his nose, looking as if he wished anyone else had been the finder.

"Nothing to be alarmed about, Eli," the chief said easily, maybe aware of Daed's tendency to be upset about the Englisch world intruding on their lives. "I thought you'd want to be up-to-date about what was going on."

"It's kind of you," Mamm said, a swift look at her husband reminding him to be hospitable. "You'll have some coffee and maybe a piece of apple pie, *ya?*"

"That sounds fine, Emma." Chief O'Brian's expression relaxed, something that was the usual result of Mamm's warm friendliness.

Sara gestured him to the sofa and took the rocking chair, waiting for him to begin and hoping it wouldn't be questions about Caleb or Rachel.

"Well, we identified the man who died," he said, setting his cap on his knees. "His name was Jase Kovatch."

"Kovatch." Daed pronounced the name carefully. "I can't say as I know him."

"No, don't suppose you would. The police did, and that's not exactly a recommendation," Chief O'Brian said.

"He'd been in trouble, then?" Sara asked.

The chief nodded. "Minor stuff, mostly. Drunk driving, petty pilfering. No family that we can find, and I can't see as anyone's going to miss him much except maybe some of his drinking buddies."

"That is a sad way to live." Mamm set a mug of steaming coffee and a big wedge of apple pie topped with vanilla ice cream on the end table next to him.

"Sure is." Chief O'Brian took a bite of pie and spoke thickly around it. "I just can't figure out what he was doing up on the ridge to begin with."

"Small-game season," Daed said promptly. "Out after rabbits, maybe."

The chief shook his head. "No gun," he said succinctly.

Sara's mind chased after reasons for the man to be out there and came up empty. This time of year, people went into the woods with shotguns, looking for small game. Bird-watchers and nature lovers were sensible enough not to wander through the woods during hunting season, especially not when deer season started next month. Then all the hunting cabins would be filled to bursting.

She realized the room had fallen silent. Chief O'Brian was looking at her.

"I can't think of anything that would take the

man up there," she said, hoping she hadn't missed a question.

"You haven't seen him around? Noticed anyone maybe taking an interest in the school, for instance?"

"No." She could only shake her head, perplexed. "Why?"

O'Brian shrugged. "I went up top today, along with a couple of men. We didn't find anything unexpected. But I noticed one thing about that place." He paused, looking grave. "It has the best view a person could have of your schoolhouse."

His words sank in, and alarm ricocheted along Sara's nerves. She didn't need to look around the room to know that they were all thinking the same thing.

Everyone wanted to believe that their corner of the world was safe. Unfortunately, danger was not limited to the back alleys of big cities. Even innocent school-children weren't safe from evil in the world.

"Now, I don't want you folks to get all upset about it," Chief O'Brian said. "If this fellow... Well, he's dead now. But I wouldn't be doing my duty if I didn't mention it, just in case."

Sara nodded. "*Danki,* Chief O'Brian. If I see any-thing out of the ordinary, I'll let you know right away."

He seemed satisfied, turning back to his pie, but Sara couldn't let go of it so easily.

Tomorrow was the semiannual auction held to sup-port the school, and every Amish person in the area, as well as plenty of Englisch, would be on the school grounds for the event. Including, she hoped, Caleb

King. She had to confront him about what he hadn't told Chief O'Brian. She must make him understand that if Rachel had seen anything, she had to speak.

THREE

"The playground certain sure looks different today, ain't so?" Caleb tried to keep his voice cheerful as he and Rachel neared the auction on Saturday. Auctions were a common way of raising money for Amish schools, valued as much for their fellowship as for their fund-raising.

Rachel clung a little tighter to his hand. *"Ya,"* she murmured.

"We'll bring something to Onkel Josiah when we leave, *ya?* Maybe a funnel cake or an apple dumpling." Onkel Josiah had declined to come, since he was still hobbling around on crutches and fretting over his broken leg.

Caleb's voice sounded unnatural, even to himself, but maybe Rachel didn't notice. At least she was staring, wide-eyed, at the tents and canopies that had sprung up overnight on the school grounds. Besides the auction going on inside the big tent, there were plenty of improvised stands selling food and drink, which seemed about as popular as the auction itself.

A couple of Englisch teenagers passed them, and Rachel shrank against him. He put a hand protectively on her shoulder, a wave of dread washing over him. He'd been so sure this move would be good for his Rachel. Instead, it seemed to be having the opposite effect.

Onkel Josiah's offer had seemed a godsend. Caleb had been so eager to get Rachel away from the sad memories of her mother. But instead of making things better…

The thought trailed off when he saw Teacher Sara coming toward them. She was holding the hand of a little girl who looked about Rachel's age.

Sara met his gaze and smiled, showing a dimple at the corner of her lips. With her rosy cheeks and those dancing green eyes, she looked hardly old enough to be a teacher, but he knew from Onkel Josiah that she was only a year or two younger than he was.

She and the little girl came to a stop in front of them while he was still trying to decide if her hair was blond or brown or something in between. As if aware of his thoughts, she smoothed her hair back under her *kapp* with one hand.

"Look, Becky, here's Rachel. Now you'll have someone just your age to walk around with." Sara's gaze met Caleb's. "This is my niece, Becky, my brother's girl. She's been longing for another girl to walk around with, instead of her brothers."

He nodded to the child, who had a pert, lively face and hair a shade darker than Sara's. Becky grinned at him and grabbed Rachel's hand.

"*Komm, schnell,* Rachel. Aunt Sara said she'd get me a treat but I must look at everything before I decide. You can help me."

Rachel clung to his hand a moment longer, but at an encouraging nod from her teacher, she let go. The two girls started off together.

"Don't get too far away from us, *ya?*" Sara cautioned.

Becky nodded, already chattering away to Rachel about the relative merits of a funnel cake or an ice-cream cone.

"Danki," he said softly. "It's kind of you to think of helping Rachel get to know your niece."

"I thought Rachel might feel more at home with a friend," Sara said. "She already knows Becky a little from school. And our Becky is such a chatterbox. She talks enough to charm a turtle out of its shell."

"Rachel isn't a turtle, but she does have a shell," he admitted, impelled by a need to explain something he didn't quite understand himself. "Her mother was sick so long—" His voice seemed to stick there. "She passed not quite a year ago. Rachel hasn't had much of a childhood."

"That must have been so hard on both of you." Sara's eyes were warm with sympathy.

"Ya." He struggled to find words. "I hoped a fresh start, away from all the reminders of her *mamm,* would help her forget about the past."

"But she can't—" Sara began. Then she paused, seeming to censor what she was about to say. "I'm sorry it's been a difficult beginning for her here."

A burst of laughter came from the auction tent. Sara glanced in that direction, smiling at the sound. "Josh Davis is a fine auctioneer. He always gets the crowd into a buying mood." She turned back to him. "There's something I need to tell you."

"Ya?" They were as isolated in the noisy crowd as anywhere, he supposed. "Has something happened?"

"The chief came to our house last night. They know the man's name now." She shot a look at the girls and lowered her voice. "Jase Kovatch. The chief said he'd been in trouble with the police before."

Caleb nodded, frowning. The death of an unknown Englischer was sad, but nothing to do with them, surely.

"The worrisome thing is that the police could find no reason for him to be up there on the cliff." She took a breath, as if she didn't want to say more. "The chief says there's nothing much up there. Nothing but a good view of the school."

She didn't say any more. She didn't need to. There wasn't an Amish person alive who didn't know about the Amish schoolchildren who'd died at the hands of an Englischer.

"That's bad, that is." He fought to speak through the tightness in his throat. "But since the man is dead, there's no call to worry, *ya?*"

Sara's expression said she wasn't convinced of that. "Maybe. But we don't know for sure. If there's any danger to the *kinner*— Caleb, don't you see you must speak to the police about Rachel's fears?"

"No." His response was instantaneous. "I won't have my child involved in this."

"But—"

He cut off her protest by grabbing her wrist. He felt

her pulse thunder against his palm and released her just as quickly.

"She is my child. It is for me to say. And I say no."

They stood so for a moment, their eyes challenging each other, and the noise surrounding them seemed to fade away. He felt… He wasn't sure what he felt.

Before he could decide, a voice called Sara's name. They turned away from each other, and he wondered if Sara was as relieved as he was.

"Teacher Sara." The speaker was Silas Weaver, leader of the school board. Behind him stood another man, an older Englischer who seemed vaguely familiar.

Silas nodded to Caleb in greeting before turning to Sara. "I need a word." He made it sound like an order.

"I will keep an eye on Becky," Caleb said. "Take your time."

He moved off after the girls, just as glad to have this uncomfortable conversation interrupted. Teacher Sara seemed to have a knack for eliciting all sorts of feelings in him, and he didn't have room in his life for that.

Sara had to push down her instinctive reluctance to talk to Silas Weaver. She didn't have a choice. He was president of her school board. Unfortunately, he also possessed a stern, disapproving temperament that didn't make him easy to deal with.

She tried to manage a smile as she joined the man. "The auction is going well, ain't so?"

He grunted, casting a disapproving gaze at the tent. "We'll be lucky to end up with enough to cover our costs for a few more months. Folks don't realize how expensive it is to run a school."

Sara was well aware of Silas's reluctance to spend money on the school other than necessary repairs. She'd had more than one clash with him and come off the loser. The other two board members seemed as cowed by Silas as his own *kinner* were.

"Well, we must hope we'll realize more than expected," she said, not eager to get into another disagreement with the man.

A grunt was his only answer. He gestured to the Englischer who stood nearby. "Mr. Foster has come to me with a proposition."

Sara nodded, answering Mr. Foster's smile with one of her own and thinking she detected a bit of sympathy in his eyes.

"Mitch, please. We don't need to be formal, and I know Teacher Sara." Foster was lean and graying, with a tanned face and a ready smile. The owner of the local hardware and sporting-goods store, he was well-known for sponsoring all the local sports teams. Not that the Amish participated in those, but a person could hardly not know about it. People in a small community talked, that was certain sure.

"See, it's this way, Teacher Sara. I heard about the trouble you folks had with finding that body and all."

Silas's look turned more disapproving, if possible. "It's not proper, an Amish teacher going about finding bodies."

She could hardly expect him to approve, but Sara wasn't sure what she could have done about it. A little edge of apprehension pricked her. Silas might well seize any excuse to replace her with someone younger and more malleable.

"I'm sorry that what happened brought attention to the school," she said.

"Nonsense," Foster said bracingly. "You couldn't help what happened. You could hardly leave the poor fellow lying there. Anyway, it made me think about your school."

She nodded, not sure where this was going.

"So the long and short of it is that I noticed the playground equipment is getting a bit dilapidated. I figured I'd like to donate the materials you need for an overhaul. Maybe add a few new pieces, as well."

Sara managed to restrain herself from jumping up and down in excitement. "That's very generous of you, Mr. Foster." She slid a look at Silas, expecting a negative reaction, and realized he was actually nodding.

"Generous," Silas echoed. "Though I'm not sure the *kinner* need all these newfangled things to play with when they should be attending to their studies."

Silas's philosophy was always that what had been good enough for him was good enough for everyone.

"Scholars seem to do better with their studies when they're able to run about and play in the middle of the day," she said. *Please,* she prayed silently.

"Sure thing," Foster said. "Everyone knows that's true. They've got to run off some of their energy. So what do you say?"

Silas gave a short nod, as if to do more would be unbecoming. "Well, if you insist, we accept. We can set up a work frolic to get the repairs done. I think Teacher Sara already has a list of what's needed, ain't so?"

Sara nodded, unable to keep a smile from her face. "*Ya,* I do." A list she'd presented to the school board at least twice with no action. "I'll get it for you."

"Fine, fine." Foster took a quick look around. "I do need to get going, but I can wait a few minutes. Or you can have your *daed* drop it off at the store."

"I'll get it right away." She spun and headed for the schoolhouse, excitement bubbling, hardly able to believe Silas had agreed to this. Maybe the thought of getting something free had outweighed his reluctance. She'd best get the list to Mr. Foster before Silas changed his mind.

She stepped inside, closing the door behind her, mind intent on the list. She took one step toward her desk and stopped, her heart giving an uncomfortable thump.

Someone stood at her desk. Not just someone—a man, Englisch, young. He wore jeans and a tight black T-shirt, and he was as out of place in an Amish schoolroom as a zebra in a henhouse.

"What are you doing here?" Nervousness lent an edge to her voice.

"Just wanted to see what the school looked like. Nothing wrong with that, is there?" His bold eyes swept over her, studying her body in a way that made her want to hold something up to shield herself from his gaze.

Sara pushed down a momentary panic. There were people, plenty of them, just a shout away. Nothing could happen to her in her own schoolroom with half the residents of Beaver Creek nearby.

"The school is closed to visitors today." She made her voice firm. "I'll have to ask you to step outside."

He sauntered toward her, his gaze never shifting. "Well, now, that's not very friendly, is it?"

"The school is closed," she repeated. She took a step back and bumped into a desk. Was it time to call out now, before he got any closer? She edged her way around the desk, feeling behind her for the door.

He smiled, as if he knew she was afraid and enjoyed it. "I know lots of ways to get friendly with a pretty girl like you." He moved to within arm's reach, and only the conviction that it would be a mistake to turn her back on him kept her from running.

"Get out of my schoolroom." She would not panic. If she made a scene... Her mind shuddered away from the thought. It would be another black mark against her in Silas's book—that was certain sure.

"Your schoolroom? So I guess that makes you the teacher, huh? Bet I could teach you some things."

He reached toward her, and panic slipped her control. She drew in a breath to scream.

FOUR

Caleb's first censorious thought at finding Teacher Sara alone in the school with an Englischer vanished when he saw the fear in her face. "What is going on?" He reached them in a few long strides, impelled by an alarming surge of protectiveness.

"Sara." He moved between them, forcing the other man to take a step back. He focused on Sara's strained face. *"Was ist letz?"*

Sara took a breath, some of the color coming back into her face. "I found this man in the schoolroom. He doesn't want to leave."

And he had frightened her. Caleb could read between the lines. Had he threatened her?

He fixed his glare on the man—hardly more than a teenager, but hardly an innocent. The way he'd been looking at Sara gave Caleb an urge to douse his head in the nearest water pail.

"Go. Now." He didn't waste words.

The stranger took another step back, wiping his mouth with the back of his hand. A flicker of bravado showed in his expression.

"I heard tell the Amish don't hit back. So how you gonna make me?"

"That's true enough." And he'd never had such a longing to break that taboo. "But there are plenty of Englisch outside who'd be glad to help us out."

He didn't bother to repeat his command. He stared until the man's gaze fell.

"Just having a little fun." His voice had taken on a whine. "That's all." He swaggered out the door, the effect ruined by the speed at which he disappeared.

Caleb turned to Sara, overcome with the need to comfort her. "Are you all right? You're safe now. He's gone."

She shook her head, turning toward him in an instinctive gesture, so that it seemed the most natural thing in the world to put his arm around her.

"It's all right," he said softly, just as he would soothe Rachel. "Nothing can hurt you now."

Sara gave a watery chuckle. "*Ach,* I must be *ferhoodled* to let the likes of that one upset me so." She drew back, as if aware of his arm around her.

He squeezed her arm in reassurance and let his hand fall, taking a step away. "It was sensible to be afraid, finding a stranger in here. Did he threaten you?"

She shook her head. "I don't suppose he meant any harm. He was just showing off, most likely."

Caleb's thoughts were busy with the man's reasons for being in the schoolroom, of all places. "Did you know him?"

Sara shook her head. "You don't think I'd be friends with someone like that, do you?"

"I'm glad to see your spirit is back." Although he

couldn't help but think Sara might be safer with a little less of that quality.

"Oh." Her eyes widened. "The *kinner*. Where are they? You didn't leave them on their own?"

"The girls are fine. Your brother and his wife took them to get funnel cakes. That's what I was coming to tell you." He hesitated. "Are you going to tell Chief O'Brian about what happened here?"

"I didn't think of that." The color came up in her cheeks again. "He said to tell him about anyone hanging around the school. I suppose I must."

He thought he understood her embarrassment. The Englischer had said something offensive to her— something she probably didn't want to repeat.

"*Ya,* I think you should talk to him," he said firmly.

Sara looked at him with a challenge in her green eyes. "That's a turnaround for you, isn't it?"

He stiffened. "It's an entirely different thing. My Rachel is a child, already having a difficult enough time of it. You're a grown woman." A fact of which he was uncomfortably aware.

Sara didn't speak, but he could see the stubborn disagreement in her face. Well, maybe that was a good thing. It would encourage him to keep his guard up with her.

By the time school started on Monday morning, Sara still hadn't talked to Chief O'Brian about her unwelcome visitor. Well, it wasn't her doing, was it? He'd left the auction by the time she went in search of him, and she could hardly seek out the police on the Sabbath. She'd have to do it, and soon, but at the moment, she needed to deal with all the chatter going on in her schoolroom.

She stood, and the buzzing stopped when she looked at her scholars, but she saw suppressed excitement on several faces. Well, maybe some serious schoolwork would get their thoughts off gossip, which she didn't doubt had been flying around the valley since Friday.

"We'll begin with reading for first and second graders," she announced, and the little ones obediently began pulling their desks into a circle. "Seventh and eighth graders will work on their written reports."

There were some sighs from the older boys, who'd rather do almost anything than write a report.

She went on to assign each of the other grades to work on arithmetic or practice spelling words, and then she sat down with the small group of the youngest scholars. The room was quiet except for the scratching of pencils and the murmur of spelling words as the third graders quizzed one another.

Concentrating on the eager little ones was a good antidote for her worries. She loved seeing their faces light up when they sounded out a new word or read a complete sentence in Englisch.

A teacher's sixth sense presently told Sara that something was wrong with the background noises. She looked toward the back of the room to discover that Lily was not only not working on her report, she was out of her chair and hanging over Johnny Stultzfus's desk, whispering away.

"Lily!" Sara's sharp tone had every pair of eyes in the room focused on her. "You will take your seat immediately, and you will also write one hundred times *I will not chatter in class.* Is that understood?"

Lily, her pretty face set in a pout, nodded.

She was justified, Sara told herself, but she hated to see all of her students looking at her with such dismay.

Relenting, she went to lean against her desk. "All right. Tell me what is so fascinating to all of you that you can't concentrate on your work."

"Please, Aunt Sara." Becky remembered to raise her hand, but she forgot, as always, that she was supposed to call her aunt Teacher Sara in the classroom. "Everyone is talking and wondering about the man who fell off the cliff."

"Did he really jump?" Johnny's question exploded out of him before she could react to Becky. "I heard he had a parachute."

"Not a parachute, dummy." Adam Weaver, seated next to him, gave him a light punch on the arm. "Nobody could use a parachute off a cliff."

"Adam, keep your hands to yourself," Sara said sharply.

"I heard—" someone else said, and a babble of voices spoke, all telling a different, wilder story.

Sara sighed. If anyone had hoped the *kinner* wouldn't learn about the body at the bottom of the cliff, they'd be disappointed. The only sensible thing was to tell them the truth so they'd stop making up stories.

"Enough." She held up her hand, and the room fell quiet. "Here is exactly what happened. On Friday, after school, I was showing Rachel's *daed* the cliff, where it looks like the profile of an old man."

Several heads nodded. They probably all knew that much.

"We saw someone lying at the bottom, and we went to see if he was hurt. Unfortunately…" She hesitated, but they already knew. "Unfortunately the man had passed from his injuries."

"Was there a lot of blood, Teacher?" Adam said with a certain amount of relish.

"No, there was not." She said it firmly and held his gaze for a moment, mindful of what he might likely repeat to his father. Some of the parents were bound to dislike this departure from the curriculum. Including, most likely, Caleb.

"The poor man was beyond help, so I went to Mr. Brown's farm and asked them to call the police. The emergency squad came and took the man away. And that's all that happened. Are there any questions?"

There were, of course, but she was able to answer them honestly without giving any gory details. Finally her scholars seemed to run out of queries.

"Now you know the facts," Sara said. "So you don't need to make up any stories about it." She paused. "Do any of you have anything else to say about it?"

She let her gaze rest for a moment on Rachel. It seemed she was about to speak. But the moment passed, and Rachel joined the rest of the class in a chorus of "No, Teacher Sara."

Sara felt oddly dissatisfied. There were too many questions as yet unanswered. Maybe they never would be. But as her scholars got back to work at last, she realized that the cheerful presence of the children was chasing any remaining shadows from her thoughts as well as her schoolroom.

It was raining when school ended, a steady gray drizzle that made Sara disinclined to rush out into it. She saw Caleb standing at the edge of the playground, waiting for his daughter.

Why hadn't he come to the door for her? She hadn't spoken to him since Saturday, although of course she'd seen him at worship yesterday. Maybe Caleb thought they'd gotten too close during those moments in the schoolroom on Saturday. Now he was eager to put some distance between them.

Sara settled down to grade papers, trying to dismiss the thoughts, but Caleb's frowning face kept intruding. She sighed. Caleb was so determined that Rachel should forget the past, but obviously he couldn't do that himself. And she suspected he was wrong in his approach to his daughter's grief, although she didn't think he'd want to hear it from her.

Forcing the troubling thoughts away, she set to work and had the correcting done in an hour. She glanced at the windows, startled at how dark it had become because of the thick clouds and the steady rain. She'd better head for home before Daed came looking for her.

Putting on her outer clothes, she glanced back at the schoolroom before locking the door. With the battery lamp turned off, the familiar room looked different. But not scary. Of course not. She locked up and started down the path toward home.

At least the rain was stopping now, but water still dripped from the trees, and wet branches sagged, waiting for her to walk into them. She moved quickly, hugging her jacket around her. It was only sensible to get to the warmth and light of home as soon as possible.

The path wound along the creek, where the water rushed over the stones, fed by the rain. She resolutely did not look toward the opposite side, not that she could have seen the cliff from here anyway. Still, if—

Her skin prickled. A sound, some alien noise, had disturbed her. She was as familiar with the usual sounds along the path as she was the tone of her schoolroom. She slowed, listening, trying to identify the sound. It was the faintest murmur, but it almost sounded like footsteps on the path behind her.

Sara whirled, staring, but no one was there. *Ferhoodled,* that was what she was, letting herself imagine things. She hurried on. She wasn't frightened exactly. She'd walked this way almost every day since she was six. But the loneliest section of the path was just ahead of her now, where it dipped into the pine woods before coming out behind the barn.

It was always dark and silent in the pines. Shadowy even on a bright day, which this surely wasn't. Well, if she didn't go through the pines, she wouldn't get home, not unless she went clear back to the school and walked home along the road.

The thought of turning and walking toward the sound she thought she'd heard made her heart quail. No, it was better to go on.

She strode into the trees, trying not to imagine things in the shadows. She was perfectly all right; in a few minutes she'd be home, and it was ridiculous to let herself be spooked.

A sound came again, from behind her and to the

right—like a body pushing through the undergrowth beyond the pines. Her heart jerked, and she forced herself to turn around, to call out.

"Is someone there?" The dense shadows swallowed up her voice.

No answer. But suddenly the bushes shook as if someone was forcing his way through them. In a moment he'd step into the clear space under the pines where nothing grew. She'd see him.

No. Sara spun and ran, her breath coming in ragged gasps, her schoolbag thumping against her hip. Were those footsteps behind her or the thudding of her own heart? She didn't know, and she wouldn't stop to find out.

She ran on, letting the bag slip down so that she could grasp the strap in her hand, with some vague thought of fending off an attack. An image of a body falling from the cliff filled her mind, accelerating her fear.

And then she broke through into the cleared ground behind the barn, which glowed with a welcoming light. She raced through the door and into the comforting presence of her startled father and brother.

FIVE

Caleb didn't stop at the end of the path as he usually did when he walked Rachel to school in the morning. The memory of her frightened cries in the middle of the night was too strong. He wouldn't relinquish her hand until they'd reached the safety of the school.

He spotted Sara almost immediately, standing by the porch, in conversation with a man he recognized as the school board head. It didn't look as if either of them were enjoying their talk.

Rachel tugged at his hand, apparently ready to join some of the other youngsters at the swings.

"Have a *gut* day." He touched her cheek lightly, wanting to hold her tight and knowing he couldn't. "Listen to Teacher Sara, *ya?*"

"I will." She hesitated. "You'll *komm* after school?"

"I'll be here," he promised. "Go on, run and play until the bell rings."

When he glanced at Sara again, she was alone and looking relieved. Catching his eye, she came toward him, smiling but not, he thought, quite as blooming as usual.

"Is something wrong?" he asked bluntly when she was close enough.

"No, not at all," she said too quickly. "How is Rachel?"

"She had another bad night." Some things he'd rather keep to himself, but if Sara were to help Rachel, she had to know. "I tried to get her to tell me what frightened her, but she wouldn't." His frustration was probably obvious.

"I'm so sorry." Distress filled Sara's face. "I hoped…" She let that trail off.

"You talked to the *kinner* about what happened, Rachel says."

Sara seemed to brace herself for his disapproval. "I felt I had to."

"*Ya,* I know," he said quickly, not liking that she expected instant criticism from him. "I understand. They'd be imagining worse if you didn't tell them."

Relief flooded her face. "I wish other parents understood that."

"Giving you a hard time, are they?"

"Not all, just a few. Silas Weaver in particular." She broke off as a buggy swung around in the lane next to them.

Her niece, little Becky, hopped down and raced off toward Rachel. Sara's brother leaned across the seat, grinning.

"Morning, Caleb. Sara, have you seen any more bogeymen since last night?"

"Very funny, Isaac." But he was already driving off.

Caleb studied her, alerted by the tension in Sara's face. "What did your brother mean?"

"It was nothing." But she rubbed her arms as if she were chilled. "I just… I went home a bit later than usual yesterday. It was such a dark day, and I thought I heard someone following me along the path."

He frowned, sensing it was more serious than she wanted to let on. "Did you see anyone?"

"Not exactly." She seemed to be trying to get it straight in her mind. "I thought I heard someone behind me, but when I looked, no one was there. Then when I reached the pine woods, I heard it again. I called out. No one answered, but the bushes moved as if someone was pushing through them. Isaac says I was imagining things. It must have been an animal."

Nothing he'd seen of Sara would make him think she was easily spooked. "An animal wouldn't sound like a person's footsteps."

She looked startled that he was taking it seriously. "No. But if it *was* a person, he had left by the time my *daed* and Isaac went out to look."

"I don't like it." His frown deepened. "Someone could have been waiting for you to leave so he could follow you. I think I'd best have a look around outside the schoolhouse, if it's all right with you."

"Ya, danki." She managed a smile. "I hadn't thought of it, but that would make me feel safer."

The school bell set up a clamor, shaken by one of the older boys who seemed to enjoy making as much noise as possible. The *kinner* came running to line up, two by two, and began walking into the schoolhouse. Sara, with a last grateful look at him, followed them inside.

Caleb waited until the school door closed behind Sara. Then he studied the building, considering. He wasn't what anyone would call a fanciful man, but he'd sensed the fear Sara felt when she talked about her walk home the previous day. The Esch farm wasn't all that far from the school, but the path was a lonely one, and it would have been dark and isolated under the trees.

He circled the schoolhouse with deliberate steps. For someone to follow Sara, he must have been hiding someplace out of sight, waiting for her to leave. A car parked near the Amish school would have been spotted instantly.

He scanned the ground beneath each of the windows, his skin crawling at the thought of someone peering in at Sara. But there was no sign of disturbance.

A windowless white frame storage shed stood behind the school building. The door was padlocked. No one could have lurked there. He began to feel foolish, prowling around the school this way, until he reached the rear of the storage shed.

Boot prints were plainly visible in the ground left muddy by yesterday's rain, and the stubs of several cigarettes littered the ground. He stared, almost wishing he could disbelieve the evidence in front of his own eyes.

But he couldn't, and he couldn't fool himself that ignoring this would make it go away.

Moving quickly, Caleb circled the schoolhouse to the door and tapped lightly before opening it. Every head swiveled toward him.

"Teacher Sara, may I have a word?"

Sara nodded, eyes widening. She gave a few quick

words of instruction to her scholars before coming to join him on the porch.

"You found something?"

"*Ya.* Behind the storage shed. Footprints in the mud that look like boots. Man-size, not a child's. And cigarette butts. Someone waited there, smoking."

Sara paled, but she didn't lose her composure. "It couldn't have been any of the scholars. Not even the older boys would do that."

The sound of a motor interrupted her, and they watched as a panel truck drove up the lane. Caleb took an instinctive step in front of Sara before realizing the truck bore the name of the local hardware store.

Mitch Foster got out and regarded them quizzically for a moment. Then he headed for them.

"Something wrong? You folks are looking upset. I was just going to get some measurements for the playground equipment materials while the kids are still inside, but if this is a bad time…"

"Not exactly." Sara looked as if she didn't know quite what to do with the man. "Maybe later would be better." She sent a questioning look toward Caleb.

He made a quick decision. "We found signs that a stranger has been lingering on school grounds. If you are going back to town, maybe you could stop at the police station for us?"

Foster looked startled but agreeable. "I can do better than that. I've got my cell phone. We'll give the chief a call right this minute."

It was done. Caleb couldn't ignore the possible danger to the other *kinner* and to Sara, no matter how little he might want to be involved. Still, it had become too serious to pretend he could. Like it or not, he'd have to tell the police chief about Rachel's nightmares.

Once again, Sara found herself and Caleb in consultation with Chief O'Brian—not in the schoolroom this time, but behind the storage shed, staring at the footprints. The muddy marks gave her too strong an image of someone standing there, watching the schoolhouse, waiting for her, and she edged a half step closer to Caleb's comfortable bulk.

"No doubt someone was here for a fair amount of time," the chief said, squatting to have a closer look. "Don't suppose it could have been one of the older boys?" He made it a question.

Sara shook her head, grateful when Caleb took it upon himself to answer.

"A scholar that age wouldn't dare. And there's not one of them would wear boots that make that kind of print. Maybe when they hit *rumspringa,* but not at this age."

For all his earlier reluctance, Caleb was clearly ready to take charge, and she was just as glad to let him. She'd hate to have to admit the hollow feeling it gave her to know her fears were justified.

The chief nodded, rising, and gestured for the young patrolman he'd brought with him to take pictures of the marks. Then he eased Sara and Caleb around the building.

Once they were seated on the steps of the porch, O'Brian pulled out a small notebook. "Now, Sara, I know this is upsetting. But did you get any glimpse of the man you say followed you last night?"

She shook her head. Did the way he phrased the question mean he didn't believe her?

"Have you seen anybody hanging around?"

"There was an Englischer in the schoolhouse on Saturday, when the auction was going on." Caleb answered again, maybe to save her embarrassment. "Sara found him. She told him to leave, but he was..." Caleb glanced at her. "He refused to leave."

The chief cast a cautious look at Sara. "Insulted you, did he?"

She nodded, hoping she wouldn't have to repeat the things the man had said.

"So how did you get rid of him?"

"I came in," Caleb said.

"I see." The chief's glance went from Caleb's stoic face to hers, which she felt quite sure was red. "So both of you got a look at him. Can you describe him?"

"I'd guess him to be early twenties," Caleb said. "He had dark hair, a thin face, a couple of those tattoos on his arms."

"He was wearing a black T-shirt," she said. "Jeans and b-boots." She looked quickly at Chief O'Brian. "He did have boots on."

The chief was frowning. "In that case, I think I know who it is. Kid by the name of Sammy Moore, it sounds like." He paused a moment. "He was a buddy of Jase Kovatch's."

Sara realized she was shaken but not really surprised. "They wore the same sort of clothes, ain't so?"

Caleb nodded. "What are you going to do?" He shot the question at O'Brian. "If Sara or the *kinner* are in danger from this man, we need to know."

O'Brian looked up at that. "Why the kids? Seems to me by the sound of things it's Sara he's interested in."

Sara held her breath. *Please, Caleb. Tell him about Rachel.*

Caleb's face was so tight it seemed the skin was stretched over the bones. "My child, Rachel, has been having nightmares about Der Alte—the cliff face. It started on Thursday night."

Chief O'Brian's face lost its usual smile. "According to the medical examiner, Kovatch died sometime Thursday afternoon."

"So." A white line formed around Caleb's lips. "My little Rachel might have seen something that day."

"What does she say about it?" O'Brian shifted his weight, looking uneasy, as if this turn of events upset him, as well.

"Not much," Caleb admitted. "All I've been able to get out of her is that she's afraid of Der Alte."

"And this started before you found the body." O'Brian sighed. "I don't like doing it, but it sounds as if I'd better talk to her."

"No," Caleb said instantly, glaring at the chief.

"She probably wouldn't open up to you," Sara said, hoping to disarm the sudden antagonism between the men. "Rachel hasn't been here long enough to get to know you, and her Englisch isn't very strong yet."

The chief looked exasperated. "What do you suggest? If the child saw something, I have to know what."

"I think Rachel might speak to Teacher Sara," Caleb said, and she could hear the reluctance in his voice.

"But I've already tried to get her to tell me what was wrong," she protested. "I failed."

"*Ya,* but that was in the schoolroom with others around." Caleb focused entirely on her, as if this were between the two of them. "I've been thinking on it. If you came to the house for supper, maybe played with her a little, even helped her get ready for bed…" Pain clouded his eyes that he had to ask for help with his child, and Sara's heart hurt for him. "That's when she always used to talk to me."

Chief O'Brian cleared his throat. "I'd be agreeable to that," he said. "Teacher Sara's as reliable as anyone I know."

They were both looking at her, but they couldn't know her thoughts. She'd gone to her scholars' homes for supper plenty of times, but never to a home with a single father. Never with a man she found herself so attracted to as Caleb.

But there was no choice.

She nodded. "All right. *Ya,* I will do it."

SIX

Caleb sat on the top step outside Rachel's bedroom that evening, listening to the sounds coming from within. So far all had gone as they'd planned. Sara had arrived in time for supper, bringing with her an apple-crumb pie.

It had been the liveliest meal they'd had around the kitchen table since he and Rachel had come to Onkel Josiah's farm. Josiah had been on his best behavior, joking with Sara and even teasing a smile from Rachel.

Afterward, Sara had insisted she and Rachel would help with the washing up. Onkel Josiah retired to his rocking chair in the living room, and Sara kept the chatter going while they washed and dried.

Now Sara was putting Rachel to bed, something Rachel had greeted with enthusiasm. He was the one who'd suggested this, so it was *ferhoodled* to feel left out and maybe even a little resentful of all the giggles coming from the room. But it had been a long time since he'd been able to make his daughter laugh.

By moving slightly, he could peer through the crack in the door and see them. Rachel was tucked in her bed, with Sara leaning against the headboard, arm around his daughter. She was reading a fanciful story about a piglet, and they both giggled over the pictures.

The story came to its happy ending, with the piglet home in its pen. His hands clenched on his knees. Now Sara would move toward the purpose of her visit.

"I like made-up stories about animals, don't you?" Sara smoothed Rachel's hair back with a gentle hand.

"Me, too." Rachel looked confidingly up at her. "Peter Rabbit especially. Daed reads it to me."

He'd read it so many times Rachel had it memorized, but she still wanted to hear it.

"True stories are fun, too," Sara said. "My *daadi* tells stories about when he was a boy and all the mischief he got into. You know the difference between a made-up story and a true one, don't you?"

Rachel wore a tiny frown, but she nodded.

"Like the story of Der Alte," Sara said, her tone casual. "The *kinner* made that up, but he's not real. It's just that the rocks look like a face, that's all."

He could see Rachel stiffen at the mention, and it took all his strength to keep from rushing in and snatching her up in his arms.

"But he is real, Teacher Sara." Rachel's voice trembled. "I saw the Old Man make the other man fall."

The words reverberated in Caleb's mind. It was what he'd suspected all along, but it was still a blow. He should have protected his little girl, but how?

Sara held Rachel snugly against her body. "Do you mean the rocks made him fall?" Her voice expressed none of the tension she must feel.

Rachel shook her head.

"Then what?" Sara stroked her hair again. "You can tell me."

For an instant he thought Rachel would clam up. Then she took a firm hold of Sara's apron. "The Old Man came to life," she whispered. "He pointed something at the other man, and the man fell over the edge." The words came out in a rush, and she buried her face in Sara's sleeve.

"Did the Old Man push the other man over the edge?"

Rachel shook her head, and relief took his breath away. At least she hadn't seen a murder. This was bad enough.

"What did the Old Man look like?" Sara asked.

Rachel seemed puzzled. "I don't know. Just like the Old Man."

"I'll tell you something I know for certain sure," Sara said. "I know it was just another person up there, not Der Alte. Maybe the two of them were friends, taking a walk. Or maybe they were arguing, and the poor man just tripped and fell. But it doesn't have anything to do with the face in the rocks."

She said it with such confidence that Rachel looked impressed. Maybe she could accept from her teacher what she couldn't from him.

"Are you sure?"

Sara nodded. "And I'll tell you why I'm sure about it. Because when my brother was younger, he climbed right up those rocks one day, clear to the top. And he didn't see anything else. Just rocks, because that's all they are. All right?"

"If you say so, Teacher Sara."

At first Caleb feared his daughter was just trying to say what she knew her teacher wanted to hear, but as Rachel leaned back on the pillow, he could see the relaxation in her face.

"Now I'm going to tell you a real story about the time I went to pick blackberries with my brother," Sara said. "And you're going to close your eyes and try to see all the things I tell you."

Sara began a story, her voice soft, the words repetitious. The tale grew slower, her tone more gentle as Rachel slid into sleep. Finally Sara eased herself off the bed. She tucked the quilt over Rachel and bent to kiss her forehead.

The simple gesture seemed to seize his heart. He got to his feet as Sara slipped from the room.

"You heard?" she whispered.

He nodded. "We'd best go downstairs and talk about it."

To say nothing of deciding what exactly they would tell Chief O'Brian.

Sara followed Caleb downstairs, her mind busy fitting the pieces together. He paused at the bottom, nodding to where his uncle slept in the rocking chair, newspaper draped across his lap.

In silent agreement, they moved into the kitchen. It was better to talk about what they'd learned from Rachel without an audience.

The kitchen was utilitarian, with no flowers blooming on the windowsills or colorful calendars on the walls. Even though the Amish didn't believe in useless ornamentation, a woman usually made her kitchen a warm, cozy place through a dozen little touches. Josiah's wife had been gone a long time now, and he wasn't one to bother with what his house looked like.

Caleb pulled out a chair for Sara at the kitchen table and sat down opposite her. She studied his face, looking for a clue to his feelings.

"At least now we know what Rachel saw." His voice was heavy with regret. "For my child to see a person fall to his death… No wonder she's been having nightmares."

"And no wonder she didn't want to say anything. I suppose trying to talk about it made it too real. But bad as it is, it sounds as if Kovatch fell accidentally, don't you think?" Sara tried to cling to the one bright spot in the whole business.

Caleb frowned. "That's not what Rachel thinks. She said the other man pointed at him and made him fall."

"*Ya,* but…" Sara struggled to make it fit. "We know he wasn't shot. It might have been coincidental, his pointing just when Kovatch tripped."

Caleb shifted restlessly in his chair, as if possessed of the need to do something, anything, to resolve this tangle. "If that's so, why hasn't the other man come forward?"

"I can't imagine." She pressed her fingers to her forehead. "To see someone fall and not try to get help for him—that's incredible."

"If the two of them were up to no good, I suppose that might account for it," Caleb said. "At least that's for the police to figure out."

She nodded. This was one situation she'd be happy to leave to the authorities. "Chief O'Brian said he'd

stop by my *daed*'s tonight to hear what I learned."
She hesitated, not sure he was going to like what else
she had to say. "Daed also insisted we must inform
the bishop, before he hears about my being involved
from someone else."

Caleb's lips tightened, but he nodded. "I can understand his wanting to explain the police being at his
house. It's not what we're used to."

Nothing about this situation was remotely common
in her usually quiet life, that was certain sure. "I'm
sure Rachel has told all she knows, and that's what I'll
say to Chief O'Brian. There's no point in his troubling
her with any questions."

"*Ya. Danki,* Sara," he added.

"As for her confusing the Old Man of the cliff with
the person she saw, that's probably natural at her age.
Most likely she heard one of the *kinner* say something
about Der Alte shortly before she saw the accident and
mixed them up in her mind."

Caleb nodded, but he didn't really look relieved.
She could hardly blame him.

"You did a *gut* job of reassuring her. I'm grateful to
you, Sara." The bleakness of his face extended to his
eyes. "I could not have done as well. I couldn't even
get her to tell me."

His pain seemed to wrench her heart. He needed
reassurance as much as Rachel had, it seemed. "Sometimes it's easier for a child to talk to someone other
than a parent, that's all. I remember telling my *mammi*
things I didn't want to tell Mamm."

"Maybe." He didn't look comforted. "My little
Rachel has had so much sorrow in her life, with her

mamm sick for so long. But at least we used to be close. Since her *mamm* died, she's been so withdrawn."

"Even when we know it's coming, death is a shock." Sara picked her words carefully. "And children get funny ideas sometimes about what caused it."

"I thought bringing her here would help her forget." The words came out explosively, and his hands clenched into fists. "Instead I made it worse."

"*Ach,* Caleb, you mustn't blame yourself." She touched his taut fist tentatively, wanting only to comfort him. "I don't think it's possible to forget the passing of those we love, even for a child." She hesitated, afraid she might be going too far, but he needed help so badly. "Have you talked with her about it?"

He seemed to draw away. "Not much." His voice was choked. "It's too hard."

Her heart ached for him and for Rachel. "I know. But it might help Rachel heal if you could talk, even a little, about how you feel."

"No." His facial expression seemed to close and his voice grew harsh. "I won't expose her to my grief. She's only a child. Don't you see that?"

"I know. I just want to help," she said, keeping her tone gentle. If he had to be angry with someone over what had happened, it might as well be her.

"I'm sorry." He rubbed his hand over his face, as if trying to chase away the tension. "I should not have snapped at you. You are the best thing that's happened since we came here. For Rachel, I mean," he added quickly.

"She's a dear child. How could I help loving her?"

Caleb almost smiled. "You have plenty of love for

your scholars. Anyone can see that. But you haven't..."
He let that sentence die out, but she suspected she knew where it had been headed.

"Haven't married?" She wouldn't hide from it, as if it had been her fault. "I was supposed to be wed once. But it seemed Tommy always had something to do first—finish his apprenticeship, save some money, get experience with a job in Ohio—and then when he did marry, it was to someone else."

It was his turn to touch her hand now. "He must have been *ferhoodled*."

She shrugged. "Folks thought I should be heartbroken. But by then, I was busy with my teaching. I found my happiness with my scholars, and I didn't look for anything else."

She still didn't, did she? She was suddenly aware of how alone they were in the quiet kitchen, with Caleb's hand clasping hers so warmly.

"I...I should go home," she stammered. "They'll be wondering why I'm so long."

"Ya." He let go of her hand and stood, turning to take her jacket from the hook on the wall. "I don't like thinking of you driving back by yourself."

"Ach, the evenings are long this time of year. It's not near dark yet, and I'm going less than two miles down the road."

He glanced at the window and then nodded, holding the jacket as she slipped it on. He paused for a moment, his hands on her shoulders, and when she looked up, his face was very close to hers, his gaze warm on her face.

Her breath caught, and she couldn't have moved to

save herself. They stood so for an endless moment. Then Caleb was turning away, opening the door for her, careful not to look at her.

"Good night, Caleb," she said quickly and hurried out of the house, her cheeks hot, trying to figure out what had just happened.

SEVEN

Sara reached the end of Caleb's lane before her brain started working again. Fortunately Star could find her way home from just about any place Sara drove her.

Small wonder her thoughts were in such a jumble. She had never felt anything like those moments when she and Caleb looked into each other's eyes. The feelings she'd once had for Tommy Miller seemed like boy-and-girl foolishness in comparison.

Sara bit her lip as she turned toward home on the narrow blacktop road. And speaking of foolish—wasn't that what she was being right this very minute? Caleb probably felt nothing more than gratitude for her help with Rachel. She couldn't build that into romance, and she certain sure couldn't let Caleb see what she felt.

Star trotted along comfortably, unconcerned with the tumult in Sara's heart. Star wouldn't blink an eye even if a car whizzed past with its horn honking, something Englisch teens sometimes did out of mischief, but there was no traffic on the road at the moment.

Sara glanced toward the western ridge. As she'd told Caleb, it wasn't really dark. The sun was just beginning to slip behind the ridge, painting the sky with a vibrant splash of pink and purple. She feasted her eyes on the sight, letting God's handiwork soothe her troubled spirit.

Whatever happened or didn't happen with Caleb would be God's will, and she would accept it. If she was meant to end her days teaching other people's *kinner,* that was still a high calling. All she could do was her humble best.

She'd nearly reached the lane to the schoolhouse when she realized that the reference book she'd intended to bring home still lay on the corner of her desk. She'd be hard put to prepare tomorrow's geography lesson for the eighth graders without it. A bright group, they constantly challenged her. She loved them for it, but she didn't want to let them get ahead of her.

With an inward sigh, she tugged on the line, signaling Star to turn into the schoolhouse lane. The flicker of Star's right ear showed the mare's annoyance at being kept any longer from her stall and her supper, but she turned obediently.

Well, this would only take a moment. Sara would still reach home well before dark. She had to admit that she'd grown a bit wary of being outside alone after dark these past few days.

The playground looked lonely without the *kinner,* but it seemed to Sara that she could almost hear the echoes of their voices. She toyed with the notion, half smiling as she thought of the generations of young ones who'd attended the Beaver Creek School. Had they all left echoes of themselves here?

Star came to a halt at the porch, and Sara slid down

from the buggy seat. She patted the mare affection-
ately.

"I'll just be a minute, no more. Then we'll go home,
ya?"

The mare's head moved, jingling the harness, as if
nodding in agreement.

Sara had the key ready in her hand, and she unlocked the door and stepped inside, letting it swing
closed behind her, her thoughts on the book. She
hadn't taken more than a couple of steps toward the
front of the room before she realized her mistake.

Outside, it was still plenty light, but in the schoolroom, with the shades pulled down as she always left
them, the darkness was nearly complete.

She took another step and walked smack into a
desk. Her breath caught. *Ach,* objects always seemed
to move from their places in the dark. She felt dis-
oriented. She'd have to feel her way back to the door
and prop it open. Then she'd have enough light for
her errand.

With her hand on the nearest desk, Sara made her
way back down the row, stretching her hand out in
front of her to feel for the door. Her fingertips touched
the wooden frame, and she slid her hand down until
she grasped the knob.

The door creaked a little as she pulled it open. Then
she heard what sounded like a rush of feet behind her,
setting her heart pounding. She spun, instinctively
shielding her face with her arm. Something hard struck
the side of her head, and pain exploded, taking her
breath away. She stumbled a few steps and fell heav-

ily, her outflung arm hitting a desk, adding another layer of pain.

Sara gasped for breath, curled onto her side, unable to move. But she had to move. Panic surged along her nerves. She had to move, had to try to defend herself. She couldn't lie here helpless. If he came after her—

But even as she fought her way to her hands and knees, she realized that the footsteps were receding, not coming closer. He was rushing out the door, his feet now pounding on the porch.

Sara lunged forward, determined to get at least a glimpse of him. She grabbed the door frame, her head spinning, and tried to focus her eyes.

He was running toward the patch of woods to the side of the school. In a moment he'd vanished, but not before Sara recognized him. It was the man who'd been in the schoolroom on Saturday.

Fresh fear trickled through her. She tried to stand, discovered her legs wouldn't support her, and sat down abruptly on the porch floor. Star, seeming to know something was wrong, whickered anxiously.

"I'll be all right," she said, more to hear the sound of her own voice than to reassure the mare. "He's gone."

But he could come back. Remembering how he'd looked at her brought a wave of nausea. Or maybe that was only the effect of the blow. She raised her hand to her head, vaguely surprised that she didn't seem to be bleeding. A lump had already risen on her head, but her bonnet must have protected her from the worst of it.

She couldn't just sit here, hoping he didn't come back. She had to get to safety.

Suppressing a moan, Sara clutched the railing and half crawled, half fell down the steps. Reaching the buggy, she clung to the edge of the seat, not sure how she was going to climb up. But if she didn't, if the man came back—

That was enough to propel her into the seat. She fumbled for the lines, a fresh wave of dizziness sweeping over her. Something roared in the distance.

Hold on. She had to hold on. She snapped the lines and clicked to Star. The mare started off at a trot, throwing Sara off balance so that she slid sideways on the seat. It didn't matter. She rested her throbbing head against the padded seat. Star would take her home.

The noise alerted Caleb. Not that it was strange to hear a siren on the country road—police after a speeder or an ambulance rushing to the hospital. Still, he couldn't deny that he'd had an uneasy feeling since Sara had left.

He stepped out onto the porch, looking toward the sound. His heart jolted. Flashing lights sped down the lane toward the schoolhouse.

Wheeling, he strode into the house. Onkel Josiah looked up. *"Was ist letz?"* He tossed his paper aside and reached for his crutch.

"I don't know. Something at the schoolhouse." Caleb grabbed a flashlight from the drawer. "I must go. You'll be all right with Rachel?"

"Ya, ya, fine. Go." Onkel Josiah waved a hand as if to hurry him.

Caleb was outside in less than a minute. No point in harnessing the mare—he could be there faster on foot.

He set off at a jog along the path, which was shorter than going clear out to the road.

And all the while he ran, the circle of light from his flashlight bobbing ahead of him, wordless prayers lifted from his heart.

Sara. He should never have allowed Sara to go home alone. If she was in danger, hurt, even worse... His mind wouldn't allow him to go any further in that direction.

Sara would be all right. She must be. It was over an hour since she'd left his house. She should have been home in no more than ten minutes or so.

But all the logic in the world couldn't help when he burst into the clearing around the school and saw the police cars pulled up at the door, their lights circling, flashing on the school, then the playground. He thundered up the stairs to the porch and burst into the schoolroom, heedless of the young patrolman who held out an arm to stop him.

"What's happened? Sara—" Before he could say more he spotted her, standing next to her father on the other side of the room. She looked pale, shaken, but otherwise whole, thank the Lord.

Ignoring Chief O'Brian and several other men who were clustered around the teacher's desk at the front of the room, Caleb hurried to Sara.

"Are you all right? What happened?" He spared a quick nod for her father, but all his attention was on Sara. She was so pale, she looked as if she'd pass out, and his heart lurched.

"I'm safe." She tried to manage a smile, but it wasn't

very successful. "Just a lump on my head and a few bruises, that's all."

"How?" He wanted to take her arm but he couldn't, not with her father right there and everyone in the schoolroom, it seemed, looking at him.

"Sara's going to be fine," Chief O'Brian said, but his ruddy face was strained. "She stopped at the school for something and interrupted an intruder." He glanced at the police photographer, who was taking pictures of the books and papers that must have been swept from Sara's desk. "A vandal, maybe."

If the chief thought this a matter of random vandalism after all that had happened, Caleb didn't think much of his intelligence. But O'Brian's warning glance suggested that he didn't want to have a conversation on this subject with an audience.

Caleb nodded slightly. Just as well not to make everything they knew public, especially since Rachel… His heart cramped at the thought of his child.

"Sara looks as if she'd be better off at home," he said.

Eli Esch broke in. "*Ya,* that is chust what I was saying, too."

"Now, folks, just take it easy. Sara agreed to come over and see if anything's missing. Isn't that right, Sara? Just as soon as the photos are done, she can take a quick check and then go off home to her *mamm.*" O'Brian turned back to his officers.

"It won't be long," Sara murmured. "I can wait."

"At least you don't need to stand." Ignoring the others, Caleb seized a straight chair that stood against the wall and brought it over to her. "*Komm.* Sit."

Sara sank into the chair gratefully. *"Danki."*

"I should never have let you drive home alone," he said, keeping his voice low.

Sara shook her head and then winced. "My fault, not yours. I stopped for a book, not thinking how dark it would be inside the schoolhouse. There was someone here. He knocked me down trying to get away."

Caleb felt sure she was trying to minimize what had happened. She must have been terrified, alone here at the man's mercy. "Did you see who it was?"

"Ya." Her voice trembled a little. "Sammy Moore. The man who was in the schoolroom at the auction."

"You told the chief?"

She nodded. "He said he's been looking for the man ever since I first told him about it."

Sara's father entered the conversation. "He hasn't been able to find him." Eli's face tightened, reminding Caleb that Sara was his daughter, and no doubt he was just as shaken by the danger to her as Caleb was about Rachel.

"Did you tell the chief what Rachel said?" Caleb asked softly. If he knew that, the chief certain sure wouldn't talk about vandalism. The Amish were used to periodic acts of vandalism against them. This was something much worse.

"Not yet. I haven't had a chance." He could see the same worry in her eyes that he knew was reflected in his.

"All right, now, Sara." Chief O'Brian waved his people away from the desk. "You just take your time looking at everything, but don't touch any more than you have to. Let me know if anything is missing."

Sara's father took her arm protectively and walked with her to the desk. She just stood there, studying everything as if making a silent inventory.

They'd have to tell O'Brian what Rachel had said. Caleb's jaw clenched. At least they could be sure now that someone had been up on the cliff with Kovatch. Most likely that someone was this fellow Moore.

Sara pulled out the drawers in her desk, her face sober. Finally she looked up.

"Only one thing is missing," she said, her pallor seeming to intensify. "The school register. The book that lists all the scholars with their ages and addresses."

Silence reined. Everyone must be thinking what Caleb was.

This was the proof, wasn't it? The man knew a child from the school had seen him that day. How long would it take him to figure out who it was?

EIGHT

Sara leaned back in the rocking chair, her aching head against a pillow. How much longer could this endless day last?

The farmhouse living room seemed crowded with Daed, Chief O'Brian and Caleb all here. She had been surprised when Caleb had been set on coming back to the house for this conversation. She'd have expected him to rush home to Rachel.

But Chief O'Brian had dispatched an officer to sit quietly outside his uncle's house, alert for any whisper of an intrusion. That seemed to allay some of Caleb's fear, although his strong face still showed strain around his eyes.

Small wonder. At the moment Caleb was recounting all that Rachel had told her. Daed shook his head, murmuring as if in prayer, his face filled with sympathy.

"Do you have anything to add, Sara?" O'Brian asked.

"No, I don't think so." She'd learned the inadvisability of shaking her head when pain stabbed her the last time she'd moved it. "Caleb heard everything from the hallway."

"And you're sure the little girl said Kovatch wasn't pushed?"

"Positive. I asked her that, and she said the 'Old Man' just pointed at him, and he fell."

O'Brian looked dissatisfied. "The thing is, if Sammy didn't push Kovatch, why is he going to so much trouble to find out who saw him?"

"It does not make sense." Daed pronounced the words in a tone which said that much of what he saw in the Englisch world didn't make sense.

"I agree with you there, Eli," O'Brian said. "Still, Sammy's not the brightest bulb in the pack. He could figure he's on the hook for threatening his pal and causing him to fall, even if he didn't push him."

"If his actions caused the man's death," Caleb began, but the chief interrupted him.

"The district attorney might come up with some charges in the accident, I guess, but with the only witness a seven-year-old child, I doubt he could make it stick. But now we've got Sammy on assault, theft, breaking and entering… That'll ensure he's not around to bother anyone for a good while. Then you folks can stop worrying about him."

"You must catch him first," Daed said.

"There's no problem about that. I've put out an alert to the surrounding jurisdictions. That old pickup of his is pretty easy to spot."

His words penetrated the fog in Sara's mind. "Pickup?"

"Sure, why?" Chief O'Brian glanced at her. "We have the license number and a description. He won't get far."

Sara shook her head and instantly regretted it. "I heard his vehicle start up. It was a motorcycle."

The certainty slid from the chief's face. "You sure of that?"

She thought of the roar she'd heard when she got into the buggy. "*Ya*. I couldn't mistake it."

The chief muttered something under his breath. "Guess he's smarter than I gave him credit for. I'll have to amend the alert."

Sara shivered a little. Maybe Sammy was not smart, but he was sly. And mean. It wasn't pleasant to think of the man on the loose. Still, surely he'd run away now that he knew he'd been identified. Wouldn't he? A flicker of panic stung her.

"The *kinner* must be protected. We'll have to cancel school for tomorrow." She started to rise, but Daed put a restraining hand on her arm.

"You are going to bed. We will take care of canceling school."

"Why don't I stop by the bishop's place?" Chief O'Brian said. "It's on my way back to town. I'll explain there's been a break-in, and we're not finished with the crime scene yet." He looked at her. "Nobody can blame you for that, Sara."

Like the bishop, the chief seemed to know everything that went on, probably including her clashes with her board president.

"That's wonderful kind of you, Chief. But I have to accept responsibility."

"Not all of it," Caleb said firmly. "And not tonight. Tomorrow, when you're better, will be time enough to meet with the board members. When you do, I'll be there."

His support warmed her, but Daed looked a bit ruffled. "It's not needed. Sara will have her family to back her up."

"Sara is protecting my daughter." Caleb's tone was firm. "It's only right that I be present to explain it."

Daed studied him for a long moment, as if judging his intentions. Then he gave a short nod. *"Ya. Gut."*

Nobody asked her what she thought of it, but at the moment, Sara was too weary to care. As Caleb said, tomorrow would be time enough to tackle all of her problems.

The next morning found Caleb back at the Esch farm again, with Rachel this time. Caleb touched his daughter's head lightly, not wanting to let her go after all the worries of the previous night. But she would be safe with Sara's family today, and he didn't want to leave her with just Onkel Josiah to watch over her while he was working, and Sara's *mamm* had suggested he bring her over.

"It's wonderful kind of you to have Rachel visit today."

Sara looked better for a night's sleep, and her smile seemed to banish the stress that he'd seen in her eyes. "We love having her here. My brother brought Becky over, so the two girls will keep each other amused. They're not used to being at loose ends on a school day."

Now the tension was back in her face, and he

couldn't be surprised. "You're worried about the effect on the *kinner* of canceling school."

"I don't want them to be afraid." She glanced at Becky pushing Rachel on the swing that hung from the branch of an oak tree. "But it would be far worse if they were at school and something bad happened."

"Ya." He couldn't let himself dwell on that subject, or he'd never let Rachel out of his sight.

"You're afraid for Rachel," Sara said, her voice soft. "I am, as well. But the chief seems convinced that Moore has run away now that he's been identified."

"Running away would be the sensible decision. But I'm not so sure he's one who thinks things through," he said.

Sara rubbed her arms, as if the thought chilled her. "Even so, he has no way of knowing it was Rachel who saw him."

He didn't find that thought much comfort. "I guess the school board agreed with the chief's suggestion of giving the *kinner* the rest of the week off, did they?"

Sara nodded, her lips tightening. "They didn't like it, that's certain sure, but the bishop spoke to them, and they agreed."

"Sara, it would be *ferhoodled* for anyone to fault you in all this." He spoke to the worry that lay behind her words. "Surely everyone can see that you did nothing wrong."

"You'd be surprised if you think that." She managed a smile. "I've already heard from Silas Weaver. The board wants to meet with me."

"When and where?" he said instantly.

Her eyes met his, and the sunlight seemed to bring

out gold flecks in the deep green. "Caleb, you don't need to get involved in this."

"I am the parent of a child in the school, so it would be my concern in any event. And everything you've done has been to protect my child. The board members need to hear that from me." He waited while Sara thought on his words.

"*Ya,* all right," she said finally. She gave a little gesture of giving in. "Silas wants to meet at the school tomorrow morning at eleven."

"I'll be there." He said it firmly enough to forestall argument.

But Sara didn't seem inclined to argue. "*Danki,* Caleb." She gave a shaky laugh. "I'll go over a little early to clear things up. The schoolroom is still a mess, and I don't want anyone to see it that way. After all, it's still my school, at least for the moment."

"They would not dream of replacing you. Where would they find a teacher who cares for the *kinner* more than you?" He touched her hand, wanting to reassure her, and couldn't seem to stop his fingers from encircling her wrist. Her skin was warm against his palm, and he felt the flutter of her pulse, light as the wings of a butterfly. His gaze met hers…met and clung. Her eyes were wide, questioning.

He let go, taking a swift step back. "I…I should get going. *Danki.*"

He drove away, not letting himself look back. What was wrong with him? He couldn't allow himself to continue like that. If anyone had noticed the way he was looking at her…

Sara was an attractive woman. A good woman. But

they didn't know each other all that well, and he certain sure didn't know what his future held. He wasn't even sure if he could love again. Maybe those feelings had been deadened during the long years of Barbara's illness.

Clicking to the mare, he turned into the lane that wound up into the woods. Onkel Josiah earned a little money by looking after some of the hunting camps when their owners weren't using them. He'd been fretting about not having made his rounds since he'd been laid up, so Caleb had promised to do that today.

He smoothed out the roughly sketched map his uncle had drawn for him. Most of the cabins were along the lane that led up into the woods, easy enough to drive the buggy to. The ring of keys was carefully marked, so that he could go inside and check each one.

The lane wound around the curve of the hill, and he had a fine view of the valley spread out below. The farmhouses looked like toys from here, surrounded by golden fields of corn not yet cut for silage. There was the schoolhouse, and in the distance down the valley he could see the scattering of houses that marked the beginning of the town.

Beaver Creek Valley was a good place. If not for all that had happened, he and Rachel might have settled down and been happy here. Of course, Onkel Josiah hadn't said anything about them staying on at the farm. Once he was well, he might expect them to leave.

He could buy a small place here, Caleb supposed. Farmland wasn't as expensive as it was some places. But not if it meant that Rachel was going to go on being afraid.

Before he could explore that notion further, he came to the first cabin on his list. Stay-a-While, the signboard read. He'd noticed the Englisch seemed to like giving names to their hunting camps.

Stopping the mare, he sorted through the keys to find the right one and slid down from the buggy seat. Onkel Josiah had said to check that the windows and doors were secure and that all was as it should be inside. Some of the cabins were furnished in a way that the Amish would find fancy, as if the owners didn't want to leave their luxuries behind even when they were roughing it.

Key in hand, Caleb reached the door, and then he realized that the key wouldn't be necessary. The door stood ajar, and the lock was clearly broken.

He hesitated, as one thought took hold. Sammy Moore was running from the police. He might think this a fine place to hide out. Chief O'Brian wouldn't thank Caleb if he set the man running again, but still, he had a job to do.

He pushed the door open cautiously, not sure what to expect. He was greeted with nothing. No sound, no movement. He stepped inside and paused, looking around.

Moore wasn't here, as far as he could tell without a thorough search. But someone had been. Several pieces of furniture lay overturned on the floor, and the gun cabinet on the wall was broken.

Caleb spread out the list his uncle had given him of the cabin's more costly contents. Even a quick look convinced him. The cabin had been stripped of its valuables. It looked as if he'd discovered what Kovatch and Moore had been doing in the woods.

NINE

Sara was at the schoolhouse well before her meeting the next day, eager to set things to rights. She didn't want anyone else to see her schoolroom in such disarray.

Her schoolroom. Would it be that much longer? Possibly not, if Silas had his way. Teaching had filled all the voids in her life. What would she do if she lost that?

Ach, don't be so foolish, she scolded. Daed would be here for the meeting and her brother also. He'd talked of asking some other parents to come, as well. And Caleb would be here. She wouldn't have to confront the board on her own.

She bent to pick up several primers from the floor, forcing down queasiness at the thought of someone handling them with evil in his heart. Smoothing out the pages, she restored them to the bookshelf. It shouldn't bother her so much. No one had been hurt, other than the bump on her head. She must thank God for that and let the rest of her feelings go.

The door creaked a bit as it opened. Sara whirled, heart pumping, a pencil falling from her hand. Caleb and Rachel stood in the doorway, and he seemed to take in her reaction at a glance.

"See, Rachel, I told you Teacher Sara would be cleaning up this morning. She'll be glad of our help, ain't so?"

His cheerful voice seemed to dispel the lingering shadows in the room.

"*Ya,* that's certain sure." Sara tried to match his casual tone. "Rachel, do you think you can find all the pencils that were spilled? That would be a big help."

"I will." Rachel let go of her father's hand. She scurried along the row of desks, crawling under them to retrieve the scattered pencils.

"I didn't know you were coming so early." *And I'm sure glad to see you.* But she wouldn't say that. Caleb seemed to be successful at pretending she was nothing to him but his child's teacher, maybe because that was what he actually felt.

"We didn't have a chance to talk when I came for Rachel." He began straightening the tipped-over desks. "I thought you'd want to know the latest from Chief O'Brian."

"Does he think Sammy Moore was the one who robbed that cabin?" Caleb's discovery surely had something to do with all of this trouble.

"Not just that." He set a visitor's chair against the wall. "The chief had his men searching hunting camps. He says every one they checked had been broken into. And they found both Sammy's and Kovatch's fingerprints, so they were both in on it."

She shook her head. "I don't understand how they

dared. Surely they knew it would be discovered soon, with hunting season starting."

"I don't suppose they thought that far ahead." Caleb frowned. "Onkel Josiah is feeling bad about it, thinking it's his fault for not checking the cabins sooner. Though how he could have done it with a broken leg I don't know."

"He's not responsible for other people's evil deeds. I suppose, if the two of them were in it together, they might have been quarreling that day up on the cliff."

"That's what the chief thinks. He's called in some volunteer help to be sure all the hunting camps in the township are checked. He says they probably have most of the things they stole hidden someplace. They couldn't sell them locally—they'd have to take them to a bigger town."

"*Ya,* I guess that makes sense." She bent to pick up a book at the same time Caleb did, and they bumped heads. She couldn't help letting out a gasp as the impact seemed to ricochet through her skull.

"Easy does it." Caleb took her elbow, helping her to straighten, and the warmth of his hand penetrated the fabric of her sleeve. "You..." For an instant he seemed to lose track of what he was saying. "You probably shouldn't be bending over at all. Let Rachel and me get things off the floor."

"*Danki.*" She was light-headed, all right, but she wasn't sure it was entirely due to her injury. "I guess that is a *gut* idea."

"Sara..." His grip tightened for a moment. Then he let go and took a step back. "I just wanted to say that Rachel has been sleeping better."

"That's *gut*." Was that really what he'd intended to say? She might never know. Caleb wasn't one to open up easily. His daughter must get that trait from him.

Rachel was absorbed in fitting the pencils back into their box, and she didn't seem to be paying any attention to them.

"Maybe talking about what happened was enough to ease her mind," she said, keeping her voice low. "Sometimes talking about things helps."

"Sometimes." Caleb seized the broom and began sweeping the dirt that had been tracked in, both by the intruder and by the police, most likely.

Obviously he wasn't convinced. Maybe he was right, but she couldn't help feeling that talking about Rachel's mother's death would do much to resolve the gap between them.

She didn't have the right to press her views, and maybe she never would. But she couldn't help caring, for both their sakes.

The sound of a vehicle in the lane distracted her. If it was Chief O'Brian, she could only hope he'd be gone before the school board members arrived. It wouldn't help her position for them to find the police in the schoolhouse.

Sara walked to the door and stepped outside, shading her eyes against the sunlight. The approaching vehicle wasn't the township police car. The pickup from the hardware store pulled up, and Mitch Foster got out.

"Good morning, Teacher Sara. I didn't think anyone would be here this morning." He glanced toward Caleb's buggy, probably thinking it was hers. "I heard about school being canceled."

"I suppose everyone is talking about it." She could hardly expect it to be otherwise. She went down the steps to join him.

"Nothing to worry you," Foster said quickly, his smile kind. "Folks are glad to see the last of Sammy Moore. And Jase Kovatch, for that matter. All these burglaries—" He shook his head. "Hard to believe they weren't caught before this."

"It is too bad. I hope folks are able to get their belongings back."

"Most of them are probably well insured." He seemed to shrug that off. "In any event, I brought the materials over for the playground repairs. Okay if I unload?"

"*Ya,* that's fine. It's wonderful kind of you. I'm sure the school board will set up a workday soon."

Apparently attracted by the sound of their voices, Caleb came out onto the porch, Rachel trailing behind him. "I'll be glad to help," he said.

But it wasn't Caleb who drew Sara's eyes. It was Rachel. The child had frozen, her eyes wide, her small face frightened. Slowly she raised her arm, her finger pointing at Mitch Foster.

"*Der Alte,*" she whispered.

Caleb froze for an instant, his mind struggling to accept what he'd heard. Then he snatched Rachel up in his arms, heart pumping furiously.

Foster's expression didn't change as he reached into the bed of the pickup. He pulled out a shotgun and aimed it at Caleb.

"Come down off the porch. Now." He gestured with the weapon. "Right over there."

Obviously he wanted to keep Caleb from seeking shelter inside the schoolhouse. Could he have done that, leaving Sara standing a scant yard from the gun? He wouldn't have to find out, it seemed.

Carrying Rachel, her face buried in his shoulder, he came down the steps. His gaze was fixed on Foster's face, but he caught a movement from the corner of his eye. Sara was grabbing for the weapon.

Foster evaded her easily. "No, I don't think so, Teacher Sara. You just back up over there with your friends."

Sara backed slowly away from the barrel of the shotgun. An image filled Caleb's mind of what Rachel must have seen—Kovatch backing away from the pointed weapon, losing his balance, arms windmilling as he fell.

"You were the one on the cliff," he said. "Kovatch was trying to get away from you when he fell."

Foster winced. "It wasn't like that. Put the little girl down."

"No." His arms tightened around his child. He couldn't do much, but he wouldn't let her go while he had breath in his body.

Sara changed direction slightly, so that she was between them and the shotgun. "Tell us what happened, Mr. Foster. It was an accident, wasn't it? We know you didn't push him."

Sara sounded so calm, as if they were talking about the new playground equipment instead of a man's life. She was gaining them time, putting off the moment at which Foster would decide what he was going to do about them.

"No, of course I didn't push him." Foster's face twisted. "I wouldn't do that. He…he just wouldn't listen to sense. He kept taking more and more risks."

"You were just trying to get him to listen," Sara said, holding Foster's attention.

"That's right." He sounded relieved that she understood. "That's how it was."

Caleb shifted Rachel slightly in his arms. He couldn't run with her. They wouldn't stand a chance that way. But if he could shove her into the buggy and slap the mare, there was a chance of getting Rachel away. *Please, God.*

"We were arguing, that was all." Foster was intent on explaining himself to Sara. "I wanted to stop. I knew it was too dangerous. At first it was so easy— just slipping a few extra items into the truck when I was shipping something out. No risk. But Jase was greedy. He didn't understand what I have to lose—my business, my good name…"

Caleb moved a cautious step closer to the buggy, measuring the distance with his eyes. Another step or two would do it.

"So his death was an accident," Sara said. She seemed to sense what Caleb was doing, and she moved slightly, keeping Foster focused on her. "You weren't to blame."

"That's right. He just fell. I wouldn't have done anything with the shotgun. I only carried it so if someone spotted me it would look as if I was out after rabbits. But he fell. I looked down, and there was nothing I could do for him. Then I saw the little girl on the play-ground, watching."

"You didn't know who it was," Sara said.

"They all looked alike. That was the trouble." His voice took on a complaining quality. "I wanted an excuse to be around the school so I could figure it out, so I thought up that business about the playground. But I still couldn't tell which kid it was, and I was afraid to get too close."

"You sent Sammy Moore to try to find out." Caleb could hear the strain in Sara's voice. How much longer could she hang on? He edged a little closer, lifting Rachel slightly. He didn't dare try to whisper an explanation. She'd be afraid.

"Sammy's an idiot. I should have known better than to trust him with anything. All he wanted was to scare you. I have to do everything myself."

"Not this," Sara said. She held out her hand to him, the way she would to a frightened child. "You weren't to blame for what happened to Kovatch. But if you harm a child…" Her voice shook with emotion. "Don't you see? That's not the kind of man you are. There's no going back from that. You'll have no future left at all."

It had to be now. Caleb lifted Rachel, his muscles tensing for a lunge toward the buggy.

At that moment Foster turned to them. Caleb's eyes met his, and he froze, his precious daughter still in his arms. Foster held the shotgun for a moment that seemed to last forever. Then he dropped it and buried his face in his hands, sobs shaking his frame.

All the breath went out of Caleb. He thrust Rachel into Sara's arms and grabbed the shotgun. He thrust it under the buggy seat. A moment later he had his arms around Sara and Rachel both, his mind filled with incoherent prayers.

TEN

It was Monday before classes resumed at the Beaver Creek School. Somewhat to her surprise, Sara was there to greet her scholars as they arrived.

Still, what else could have happened? Silas might have made more of a fuss with the other board members, but since he was the person who'd supported Mitch Foster's proposal about the playground, he'd apparently decided that the least said, the soonest mended.

Even as she greeted each scholar and answered parents' questions as briefly as she could, Sara realized she was watching for Caleb and Rachel.

She'd thought, in those moments when they'd held each other, that they'd expressed something more than relief that they were all still alive. But since she hadn't seen anything of Caleb since then, it appeared she'd been wrong.

"So, did you hear that the police caught up with that Sammy Moore?" Her brother helped Becky down from the buggy seat and leaned across to ask the question.

"No. Where did you hear that?" Relief chased the final remnant of apprehension from her thoughts.

"I had it from Chief O'Brian himself. He hailed me when I was coming through town and said to let you know. State police arrested him out on the interstate, he said. So you don't need to worry."

"I'm not worrying." She really wasn't. In those terrible moments of facing the shotgun, she'd known what it was to trust in God's care, living or dying. Whatever happened, it was God's will.

"Teacher Sara, might I talk with you for a moment?"

Her breath caught at the sound of Caleb's voice, and she struggled to greet him and Rachel normally. "*Ya,* of course. I'm glad to see you this morning, Rachel."

Rachel looked up at her, a smile lighting her small face. "Teacher Sara, guess what? Daed says that I can go to Becky's house to spend the night on Friday."

"*Ach,* I'll get no sleep that night for all the giggling," Isaac said, grinning at her. "We're sure glad you'll *komm,* Rachel." He snapped the lines, and his buggy rolled on. Rachel and Becky ran off, hand in hand, toward the swings.

"She is looking very happy this morning," Sara said, watching her. "Any more nightmares?"

"Not one." Caleb touched her elbow lightly. "Do you think if we walked around the side of the building we could talk while you watch the *kinner* on the playground?"

"*Ya,* of course." She tried not to speculate as to what Caleb had to say. *God's will,* she reminded herself.

They stopped in a spot where the autumn sunshine reflected off the white schoolhouse, warming them. She glanced up into his face, not sure what she was reading there.

Dear Reader,

Writing a suspense story set in an Amish community carries with it a set of challenges, since nonviolence is such an integral part of Amish faith. Maybe that's why we as readers find the stories so intriguing—it's a sharp contrast between the peaceful, pastoral lives of most Amish and the sometimes violent outside world.

Sara Esch is a compilation of many teachers I've been fortunate enough to know—people who are dedicated to the welfare of the children entrusted to their care, even to the extent of risking their lives.

I hope you enjoy my story. I'd be happy to send you a signed bookmark and my brochure of Pennsylvania Dutch recipes. Just email me at marta@martaperry.com, check in with me through my website, www.martaperry.com, or my Facebook page, www.facebook.com/martaperrybooks, or write to me at Love Inspired, 233 Broadway, Suite 1001, New York, NY 10279.

Blessings,
Marta Perry

Questions for Discussion

1. Did you understand Sara's special concern for Rachel in the opening of the story? How have you seen children react when they're afraid to talk about something?

2. Caleb's initial reaction to Rachel's nightmares was to blame them on the teacher. Did you understand his reaction, even though you might feel he was wrong?

3. Did you sympathize with Caleb's struggle to protect his child? Did you think he was right or wrong to try to keep her from talking to the police? Why?

4. The scripture verse for this story has been one of my favorites since I was a child. What special meaning do you find in these words?

5. Why is it so difficult to follow a belief in nonviolence in today's world? Do you sympathize with the Amish principles or feel they are wrong? Why?

DANGEROUS HOMECOMING

DIANE BURKE

I would like to thank Marta Perry and Kit Wilkinson for the opportunity to share this anthology with them, and I sincerely hope I held up my end of the task.

I would also like to thank Tina James, editor extraordinaire, who uses her talents to teach me how to be a better writer.

As water reflects a face,
so a man's heart reflects the man.
—*Proverbs* 27:19

ONE

The paper shook in Katie Lapp's trembling fingers. She read the message. Dread crept over her like an encompassing fog.

Please, Lord! Not again.

Her eyes made a sweeping glance of the land between her white clapboard house and the barn.

Nothing out of the ordinary.

The sun, beginning to rise on this crisp autumn morning, shed light on the harvested, empty fields. Katie's eyes searched every shadow, every tree.

No one was there.

She looked back at the paper and resisted the urge to drop it like she would a poisonous snake. It had been nailed to the post of the house steps. Just like the first two.

Katie's heart hammered. Her pulse quickened. A familiar tightening seized her chest and her breathing became more difficult. She slid her hand beneath her white apron and withdrew an inhaler from the pouch she had pinned to her dress.

Calm down. Remember what the doctor said. Stress will only make your asthma worse.

She clutched the inhaler in her right hand. Her other hand, the note tightly clenched in her fist, fell to her side. Hating her dependency on this medical necessity, she tried to prevent the impending asthma attack by using mind over matter. She forced herself to slow her short gasps of air and concentrated on each and every breath.

Katie closed her eyes. Although she tried to think of nothing but pulling air into her lungs, the threatening word on this third note had branded itself on her mind.

Her chest continued to tighten. Each breath was now an effort.

Please, Lord, I need to calm myself. Grant me peace.

She had to distract her thoughts from the paper still clutched in her hand.

Katie closed her eyes and tried to picture the large pond at the edge of her property. She willed herself to remember the feel of the sun on her face. She tried to remember the feel of the breeze against her skin.

Breathe in.

Now slowly exhale.

That's right. You can do it. Again.

In...

God surrounded his children with beauty and tranquility no farther away than nature. If she could just stop being so afraid...

Out.

Katie could almost smell the clean scent of a freshly mowed field, almost hear the sound of water lapping against the shore.

Peace filled her body and the painful constriction in

her chest began to ease. Her heart no longer raced. Her lungs no longer made her fight for breath.

With God's help, all things are possible.

With a sigh of relief, Katie shoved the inhaler into her pouch along with the note, which had started the whole asthma thing in the first place. She had chores to tend to. She didn't have any more time to waste on things she couldn't do anything about.

What else could she do? Report a scrawled word on a piece of paper to the police? Somehow she didn't think they would take it seriously. Tell the bishop? She knew that was exactly what she should do, particularly after what had happened to her fields, but she couldn't bring herself to do it.

The bishop had been trying for the past year to persuade her to remarry. He did not approve of a widow living alone and trying to run a farm.

Katie glanced at the puckered skin on her left wrist. Jacob was dead and he'd never be able to hurt her again. The redness from the burn had faded over the past year; the scars, both physical and emotional, had not.

No. Marriage was not a consideration. Not ever again if she had anything to say about it.

Entering the barn, she lit three oil lamps, basking the interior in a warm yellow glow. She opened the slide latch to the stall, put a halter on the closest horse and then repeated the process for the next two horses. She gathered the leads and guided them out of the barn, turning them out into the paddock.

When she returned to the barn, Katie placed the mouth of her wheelbarrow opposite the open door to make it easier to push the load outside. Grabbing her pitchfork, she mucked out the first stall. But as hard as she worked, she couldn't draw her mind away from the note crumpled in her pouch.

Who would do such a thing? Why?

Was there any possibility it might be a teenage prank? Even in *rumspringa,* when Amish teenagers were known for their less-than-stellar behavior, it would be out of character for any of them to purposely frighten a widow. She knew all of the teenagers in her small district. She shook her head. No. None of them could do such a thing.

Besides, the destruction of her crops was not a prank. It was a warning. Fear shivered down her spine. A warning she took seriously. She just didn't know what to do about it.

A shaft of morning sunlight filtered through the open door announcing the arrival of dawn. Katie doused the lamps. As she returned to her chores, the note in her pouch called to her as surely as if it had a voice. Unable to ignore it anymore, she withdrew the wrinkled paper and read it again.

A frown pulled at the corners of her mouth. How could one simple word make her so afraid? One word chill her to the bone? She ran her fingers over the crude block letters and read the word aloud.

"'Die!'"

"I hope you don't mean that."

At the sound of his voice, Katie spun around with the speed of a toy top.

"Joshua!" Her eyes widened and she couldn't hide her surprise. "What are you doing here?"

"That wasn't exactly the greeting I expected." Joshua

Miller chuckled and stepped closer. "*Guder mariye,* Katie. I'm sorry if I startled you."

The sleeves of his blue shirt were rolled up to his elbows. Blond hair poked from beneath his straw hat, fell over the back of his collar and dusted his forearms like corn silk in the fields.

"Here, let me help you." He approached with speed, placed his hat on a nail and, before she realized what had happened, he'd taken the pitchfork from her hands.

She didn't know how to react to his sudden presence in her barn or what the proper thing to say might be after he'd been gone so long, so she said the lamest thing that popped into her head.

"When did you return?"

"Last week. I'm staying with my parents," he said. "I can hardly believe how much the town has grown. The Englisch have made themselves a home in Hope's Creek. I see there are two banks now, a pharmacy, a dry cleaner. I even saw a garage at the end of Main Street that repairs their broken automobiles."

He turned his attention to mucking the stall. "What do you think of all the changes? It isn't just an Amish community anymore, is it?"

Katie shrugged. "Everyone I've met has been nice enough. We are in the world, Joshua, even if we strive not to be worldly."

She couldn't help but watch his muscles ripple beneath his blue cotton shirt as he lifted the straw and threw it into the wheelbarrow. Her cheeks flooded with heat when he caught her staring at him and grinned knowingly. Quickly, she averted her eyes.

"Are you staying or just visiting?" she asked.

Katie didn't know what surprised her more, her boldness at asking his private business or the fact that she was curious about the answer. She didn't *really* care. She avoided men whenever possible. All men. Even a man who used to be her best friend in what felt like a lifetime ago.

The three of them, Joshua, Jacob and she, had gone everywhere together. They'd fished in the nearby pond. They'd played softball in the school yard. They'd raced buggies during *rumspringa.* And many times they'd sat together under the willow tree and shared teenage problems and secrets that they knew the adults around them just couldn't understand.

Was that only a few years ago?

When had Jacob become a drunkard and a bully? Before or after their wedding? Were the signs always there, and in her youth and the throes of first love she had simply ignored them? Could her judgment of a person's character have been so wrong? If she had made a mistake in judgment, she had paid dearly for it.

"I'm back to stay." Joshua stopped what he was doing, leaned on the handle of the pitchfork and smiled at her. "It was time for me to come home."

For just an instant, Katie couldn't tear her eyes away. His sturdy, masculine build revealed he wasn't a stranger to hard work. Joshua had left Hope's Creek, Pennsylvania, a shy, gangly teenager. He had returned a man.

"You've been gone a long time."

It was simply a statement of fact. Why had she laced her words with a disapproving tone? Maybe because selfishly there had been a hundred times in the past few years she could have used the presence of her best friend. She lowered her eyes and chided herself. Joshua didn't know the things that had happened—and never would if she could help it. It wasn't fair to blame him now for not being around to help.

"I admit it's been a long time. Three years. Can you believe it?" That familiar dimple she had always teased him about appeared in his left cheek when he grinned. "It took a lot of time for my cousin to mentor me in carpentry. He threw some furniture making into the mix. I can fix a roof, build a stall or fashion a chest. I can do a little bit of everything now, I suppose."

She smiled at the welcome sound of his laughter. How long had it been since she'd laughed?

Joshua looked at her intently, his mouth twisted into a frown.

"Is everything all right, Katie? You don't seem like yourself. You're as skittish as an unbroken mare."

"Don't be foolish. Of course I'm all right. I'm just surprised to see you, that's all."

She was glad he didn't press the issue. But he was right. She couldn't settle her nerves, not for weeks now. She constantly had that eerie feeling that someone was watching her but she didn't ever see anyone nearby. She supposed the tension was starting to show. Forcing a smile to her face, she looked up at him. Warm chocolate-brown eyes stared back at her.

"What brings you back to Hope's Creek now?"

"When Daed took ill, I came to help Mamm. But I think it was just a ruse to get me home again, because as soon as I got here, Daed got better and started tending the fields again on his own."

They both chuckled. Katie remembered how close Joshua—the only son—had been to his parents.

"I'm surprised you didn't stay on the farm in the first place. I don't remember you ever wanting to work with wood."

Joshua shrugged and his grin slid away. An unidentifiable emotion flashed through his eyes. Apparently Joshua had secrets of his own. Wanting to alter the sudden tension in the barn, she tried to steer the conversation in a new direction.

"Which do you like better?" Katie asked. "Carpentry or furniture making?"

"Both. I have found that God's blessed me with the ability to know exactly how a piece of wood should be used."

"Prideful, Joshua?" she taunted.

"Thankful, Katie."

She colored at his gentle scolding.

"That's why I'm here," he said. "I heard Levi was looking for someone to build new stalls and make some repairs on the house."

Katie nodded to affirm his words. "*Ya*, that is true."

"I've come to ask for the job."

She tried but she couldn't give him her full attention. She couldn't shake that uneasy feeling that never seemed to leave her anymore. Her eyes darted around the barn, searching, second-guessing every shape and shadow. Was the person who left that note still here?

"Katie!" The sharp tone and puzzled expression on Joshua's face drew her attention.

"What?" She offered him a weak smile. "Were you talking to me? Sorry. My mind must have wandered."

"Who would have ever thought I'd be asking Levi for a job, heh?" Joshua's grin returned. "He was always just Jacob's pesky younger brother following us around. Now he's helping you run the farm and I'm asking him for a job. God has a sense of humor, *ya?*"

She glanced over her shoulder. Someone *was* crouching in the shadows. Her heart pounded in her chest and fear seized her breath. She squinted her eyes and stared hard into the back corner of the stall. She could barely make out the form.

"Someone's there!" She couldn't hide the trembling in her voice.

"Where?" Joshua frowned and looked in the direction she was pointing. He stepped inside the stall and disappeared for a moment into the shadows.

Katie thought her heart was going to stop beating.

When he appeared again, he held up a large bag of oats and a metal bucket. "Is this what frightens you?"

Katie stared at the objects in his hands and embarrassment flooded her cheeks with heat. "Levi should be here shortly. You're welcome to wait and speak with him about the work if you'd like." She held out her hand for the pitchfork. "I will finish my chores now."

Joshua studied her intently. When he spoke, the timbre of his voice was calm and soothing to her already frayed nerves.

"What kind of man would I be if I sat idly by while a woman mucked out a horse's stall?"

"Nonsense. Give it to me." Katie extended her hand.

He drew his arm away. "I will gladly finish the job I started."

"I don't need a man to do chores that I am perfectly

capable of doing myself." The instant the words flew out of her mouth, she knew she'd made a critical mistake. She could tell from the surprised look on Joshua's face that he hadn't expected this reaction from her. But she couldn't help it. Her eyes flew to the twisted flesh on her left wrist and her mind went to all the scars hidden beneath her clothing. She hadn't meant to snap at Joshua. Remorse filled her gut. Tears burned the back of her eyes.

But no man was going to order her around or use brute force to make her do his bidding. No man...not ever again.

Joshua stepped back in surprise. This wasn't the gentle, happy, spirited girl he remembered. Her blue eyes no longer held the sparkle of a lake on a summer's day. Now there was a darkness in them he didn't recognize. She appeared wary, suspicious...frightened?

Something was wrong. But he'd been gone a long time. It wasn't his place to push.

Katie's hands stayed in constant motion plucking at the string of her *kapp,* fiddling with the edges of her white apron, sliding up and down the handle of the pitchfork.

Joshua frowned.

This was Jacob's wife—Jacob's widow—and the three of them had once been the best of friends. What kind of friend would he be now if he turned a blind eye to her obvious distress? Whether she liked it or not, he was going to get to the bottom of things. Amish took care of their own. How could she expect him to do anything less, no matter how long he'd been away?

"Katie?" He kept his voice low and steady as he would if approaching a frightened animal. The moment he took a step toward her, he saw her entire body tense.

He was right. She *was* scared.

Of him? How could that be?

"Many things have changed in my absence," Joshua said. "But I never thought I'd see the day when the Katie I knew would lie."

She flinched as if he'd struck her and she looked away.

"You are not fine. Why do you tell me that you are?"

Maybe the stories he'd heard on the Amish gossip route had been true, that she was in danger of losing her farm. He could understand that causing her stress. But where had the fear come from?

One look at the silky blond strands of hair peeking from beneath her *kapp,* the clear, satiny smoothness of her skin, the natural blush of her cheeks and the pout of her lips, and Joshua felt all his old feelings come rushing back. He knew he should let someone else help her with her problems and he should run in the opposite direction. He remembered *everything* about their youth, and the pain still cut deep. He'd opened his heart to her once. He had told her that she was the only girl for him. He could still hear the tinkling sound of her laughter in his mind.

He knew she hadn't meant to be unkind. They'd been children, a year before their teens. She'd thought at first that he was teasing her. He remembered the look in her eyes when she'd realized that he might not be fooling around. The confusion. The sympathy. And then the pity. He could bear that least of all.

His stomach clenched as the pain of that memory flooded back.

He remembered what he had done. He had thrown his head back and laughed as loud as he could at the time. He had needed to convince her that she'd been right and that he'd been joking. It was the only way to save face and hold on to her friendship. It was the only way to erase the pity he had seen in her eyes.

A shudder raced through him.

Well, he wasn't a boy anymore. He knew better than to ever open his heart to her again—or any other woman right now. Teenage angst had been difficult enough. Now, though, he was trying to get his business off the ground and didn't have the time for courting.

He watched her gaze everywhere in the barn except at him and took the opportunity to study her profile. He smiled at the touch of color in her cheeks. He watched as her even, white teeth chewed on her lower lip. He allowed his eyes to slide down the gentle slope of her neck.

He inhaled deeply and forced himself to look away. No, he couldn't let himself have feelings for Katie. He had no desire to find out what adult rejection felt like—particularly from the girl he used to love.

As an adult he had become more adept at masking his feelings. He had to call on those skills at the moment as embarrassment and attraction rushed through his body.

He'd heard about the way Jacob had fallen to his death during a barn raising. He'd even heard the rumors racing through the Amish grapevine that Katie had been physically treated poorly by her husband. He had brushed that off as mere gossip. Jacob could never have hurt Katie. Could he?

But now he wasn't so certain when he noticed her skittishness. Her wariness and the flashes of fear he saw in her eyes.

Could the rumors hold any truth? And if they was true, then Joshua also needed to add guilt to his list of hidden feelings. Knowing the harm his actions—or inactions—had caused years ago, how could he ever ask Katie's forgiveness now? He didn't think he could bear the censure he was certain he'd see in her eyes if she ever found out.

He knew he was the last person on earth that Katie should rely upon right now but he also knew he was the last person on earth who could turn and walk away. He'd just have to keep his emotional distance. He'd have to treat her like a treasured friend, which she was and had always been, and nothing more. He was sure he'd be able to do that, and he totally ignored the warnings in his head telling him that task would be harder than he thought.

Silence stretched between them for several uncomfortable seconds.

"When I entered the barn, you seemed upset and shoved something into your pouch." Joshua nodded, his eyes connecting with her blue cotton dress. "Let's start there. What is it that has upset you? What is it that you are trying to hide?"

"It's nothing for you to concern yourself with." She hesitated for a moment as though she had realized he had done nothing to incur her curt tone, and with a soft smile and softer voice she said, *"Danki."*

He didn't want her thanks. He wanted answers to his questions.

With his left hand, he tilted her face and locked his gaze with hers. "Katie." He allowed his tone to voice his question...and his command. Without speaking another word, he turned his right palm up and waited.

She stepped away from his touch. Her eyes were filled with suspicion and wariness. Although he knew he hadn't done anything wrong and couldn't possibly be the reason for the emotion flashing in her eyes, he still felt a twinge of pain at her rebuff.

She surprised him when she reached into her pouch and placed the balled-up note in his hand.

He opened the wrinkled paper and frowned. "I don't understand. Where did you get this?"

"It was posted to the porch railing this morning."

"Do you have any idea who did it?"

Katie shook her head.

She offered a nervous laugh. "It isn't the first one. Nothing ever comes of them."

Joshua tried to keep shock from registering on his face. He kept his tone calm but inside his blood boiled. "How many of these notes have you received?"

"That is the third one in a month's time."

"What have you done about it?"

Katie shrugged her shoulders and gave him a puzzled look. "There's nothing to do."

"Come with me." He clasped her hand and pulled her behind him.

"Wait! Stop! Where are we going?"

She dug her heels into the ground. He stopped so abruptly that the change in momentum made her crash into him. His hands clasped her arms and he helped her steady herself and regain her balance.

The unexpected closeness caused a tension to hang in the air between them.

Joshua immediately released her but his stern tone left little room for objection.

"I don't know why you are fighting me. Why won't you let me help you? I am not going to go away and pretend that nothing is happening here."

Removing his hat from the nail, he put it back on his head, spread his feet and crossed his arms, prepared to do battle if necessary.

"If you do not come with me, Katie Lapp, then I will go myself."

She looked as if she was going to bolt at any moment, yet despite her vulnerability he sensed an inner strength he'd never seen in her before as she stood her ground and stared him down.

"Go where?"

"To the police."

"You seemed smarter when you were a boy, Joshua." She put her hands on her hips and assumed a stance. "When do the Amish run to the police?" she asked. "Have you been gone so long that you have forgotten our ways?"

"When something evil and beyond our control comes to our door," Joshua replied. "I am not too proud to ask for help when I need it."

"*Ya,* and I am certain the police will find a word scrawled on a piece of paper quite sinister. What are you thinking?"

"I am thinking that you are a widow living alone.

You should have reported the first note and didn't. Have you told the bishop or any of the elders?"

Katie lowered her eyes.

"That's what I thought. You have done nothing to protect yourself. I am your friend, Katie. I was Jacob's friend. It is my duty to step in and help. That is what I am thinking!"

Katie watched him carefully and he noticed she rubbed her left wrist.

"Did I hurt you when I pulled your arm?" Instantly, he crossed to her. His heart pounded in his chest and his pulse raced. Though his words had been harsh, he'd thought his touch gentle. Still, had he hurt her? How would he live with himself if he had done such a thing? Before she could move away, he took her hand in his and turned her palm up for a closer look.

His breath caught in his throat the second he saw the scars on her wrist. His eyes widened as his gaze flew to her face.

"How did this happen?"

Katie sighed deeply and lowered her eyes. "It is not important." She removed her hand from his. "It happened a very long time ago, Joshua, and I don't think about it anymore." He saw her cringe and knew her conscience was scolding her for her lie.

Joshua didn't push for more information. He knew Katie would only pull more inside herself if he tried. She would have to tell him in her own way, in her own time, and he would have to be patient.

But he was more certain than ever that Katie needed a friend.

Now he knew why God had put it so strongly on his heart to return to Hope's Creek.

Joshua needed to discover who was behind the threatening notes, even if it meant he would have to maneuver through the minefield of Katie's wariness and pride. He was determined to protect her from any danger—and that protection started now.

TWO

"Joshua! I heard you were back. For once the gossip is true." Levi Lapp walked leisurely into the barn and then stopped. His eyes darted from Katie to Joshua and back again. "Am I interrupting something? Is there a problem?"

Katie could feel the intensity of Joshua's stare as he waited for her to answer her brother-in-law.

"No problem, Levi. We were just talking. Joshua really came to see you."

Levi smiled. "It is good to see you again, my friend. But if you were looking for me then why didn't you stop by my house? It would have been easier to find me, don't you think?" The smile on Levi's face did little to ease the awkwardness between the three of them.

Levi had never been Joshua's friend. He had dogged Jacob's every footstep and pushed himself into the older trio's time together with annoying regularity. But it certainly would do him no good to remind Levi of that when Joshua was here to ask for work.

"It is good to see you again, too, Levi. I was told you come every morning to help Katie with the farm.

I thought I might talk to you before you started the chores."

Levi tucked his thumbs into his suspenders. "*Ya,* 'tis true. I was surprised that Jacob left the farm in Katie's name. It is our family farm. He should have known I would have taken good care of her if anything happened to him." Levi shrugged. "And that is what I do. I split my time between the farm I purchased when Jacob inherited this land from my parents, and there is no reason I can't continue to help you." He nodded in her direction and then caught Joshua's eye. "I do not wish to be rude but there are many chores to be done and I do not have the time for idle chatter. But I am sure if you join us for church services Katie will extend an invitation for Sunday dinner."

Both men glanced her way and Katie nodded.

"*Gut.* I look forward to hearing what you have been doing these past years and you can tell us about your cousin's district."

"That is kind of you, Levi. *Ya,* I will come." He smiled. "But I came here this morning to lighten your load. I heard you are looking for a good carpenter and I am looking for work. Maybe we can be a help to each other."

Levi stared hard at Joshua for a moment before he spoke.

"*Ya,* I remember hearing that you became a carpenter and I am looking for someone." Levi clapped Joshua on the shoulder. "It will be good for us to work together. When can you start?"

"Right away."

"*Gut,* come with me and I will show you what needs to be done."

Levi led the way out of the barn. When Joshua didn't immediately follow, Levi looked back over his shoulder and shot Joshua a puzzled look.

"Katie has something she needs to tell you." Joshua looked at Katie and waited.

Levi looked her way. "Is this true?"

If she had had a pie in her hand, she might have thrown it at Joshua. Why couldn't he mind his own business?

"He is Jacob's brother, Katie. He is family. He has a right to know."

Knowing Joshua was not going to budge on this issue, she brought Levi up-to-date on all three notes.

"Why didn't you mention this to me?" Levi asked. "Particularly since it was only a short time ago that someone set fire to your fields."

Joshua looked shocked at that revelation.

"Please, Levi. I think Joshua is making it more than it is. The fire in the fields was deliberately set. It was evil and intentional. I can't believe that someone so diabolical would suddenly stoop to something so simple and childish as scrawling a word or two on a slip of paper. They are vastly different incidents and I find it hard to believe the two are connected. Still, I have not been foolish. I have been cautious and alert just in case."

"We should go to the police," Joshua said.

"The police?" Levi shook his head. "I see no reason to bring them in on this. Katie is probably right. The two incidents are most likely not related."

"You aren't going to do anything?" Joshua looked astonished.

"Of course I am. But I am not going to take it to outsiders. We can handle this situation on our own, *ya?* I will bring it to the bishop. He will decide what should be done."

Joshua nodded his acceptance.

"Now, come," Levi said. "Let me show you what needs repair."

A week passed without incident. No more notes. No more feelings of being watched. The bishop had made her promise to let him know if anything out of the ordinary happened again. When nothing did, Katie relaxed in the knowledge that she had probably been right all along. The fire in the fields had been an isolated incident, and the notes…the notes were of no importance.

Life returned to normal, if normal was having Joshua work on the farm each day.

He didn't go out of his way to talk to her or interfere in her daily chores. He simply nodded with a smile when he arrived and went straight to work in the barn. When she took him a warm cup of apple cider to cast off the autumn chill, she didn't know whether to be happy or upset that he accepted the drink, thanked her and went back to his work as if she didn't exist.

She decided she was happy that he kept his distance. She didn't want to get involved in any way with any man. Especially Joshua.

But…

She couldn't keep her eyes from straying to the barn and trying to catch a glimpse of him passing the door now and then. She couldn't keep the smile from her face when he ate the slice of pie she'd given him at lunch today as if he'd never tasted anything so good. She couldn't keep her mind from wandering to childhood days of wading in the pond and fishing and taking long walks and talking.

Reluctantly, she had to admit that she had sorely missed her friend.

But every time she allowed herself to remember how close they had once been, she would also remember Jacob, and her trip down memory lane would slam to a halt.

Standing in the yard, she had been so lost in thought she didn't hear the buggy approach and almost stepped in front of it. She pulled back not a moment too soon. Shielding her eyes against the morning sun, she tried to see who was inside.

"*Guder mariye,* Katie."

It had been a good morning until Joseph arrived.

God forgive me for my unkind thoughts.

"*Guder mariye,* Joseph. Levi is in the field."

"I have not come to speak to Levi, Katie. I have come to speak to you." He climbed down from the buggy. "You know why I am here."

"*Ya,* Joseph, and nothing's changed. I do not wish to sell my land."

Joseph removed his black felt hat. "I thought you might have changed your mind after Levi returned from the market. I am sure you did not receive the income you expected after losing half your crops in that unfortunate fire. Have they found out who set the fire?"

Katie didn't want to be disrespectful of the older man

but his presence on her land and his fake friendliness made it difficult for her to hold her tongue. She knew he only wanted to seize her property.

"You know the same as I do, Joseph. I lost more than half my crop. And no, they have no idea yet who did it." She shifted the basket of eggs she carried to her other hip, redistributing the weight. "You'll have to excuse me, Joseph. I have baking to do."

"If you do decide to sell, I will give you a fair price. I do not want you to sell to the Englischer. Your land abuts mine. It is only right that you let me buy it. The Englischer will not farm the land. He most likely will level everything and build apartments or condominiums or, perhaps, a massive housing development. I cannot allow that to happen."

Joseph reached out and patted her forearm.

Katie startled and instantly stepped away.

His mouth twisted as though he had bitten into something distasteful and he drew his hand back. "Please... if you sell, let Amish land remain in Amish hands."

Katie looked Joseph in the eye. "I don't know how many ways to say it, Joseph. I am *not* selling my land. Not to you. Not to the Englischer."

Joseph placed his hat back on his head. "That is *gut*. I know the astonishing price the Englischer offered to me to buy my land and I've made discreet inquiries of others that also received offers for their land. If he offered you the same, then I would understand how that could appeal to a widow trying to make ends meet on her own."

"I am not alone. I have Levi, and Joshua is making repairs, and Esther buys my eggs and my pies for her bed and breakfast. And you know that Esau and Matthew helped Levi with the harvest."

"*Gut.* I am happy that you will be staying on the land." He climbed into his buggy. "But if you should change your mind…" He clicked the reins and turned his horse around.

Katie watched him leave and disturbing thoughts filled her mind.

If he really knew how much she wanted to sell…how hard it was each day to keep things afloat…how unsure and afraid she was, then he wouldn't have left so easily.

But if she sold the land, where would she go? What would she do? Her parents had left the community right after she married Jacob, and moved to the Amish retirement community in Florida. Her father said his bones protested too much with each passing winter. She certainly wasn't ready to move into a retirement village, so moving back with her parents was out.

The fire chief's words last month that the fire in her fields had been deliberately set still caused an icy chill to crawl up her spine.

Who was doing this to her and what did they want? *Die.*

The memory of the word scrawled on the last note actually made her skin crawl. She did not want to think that anyone who knew her would say such a terrible thing, let alone mean it. She was unsettled and couldn't help but wonder what might happen in the months ahead.

A shiver raced through her and she clasped her arms around her waist.

Katie continued to watch the buggy until it became

nothing more than a speck on the horizon. She almost had to stop herself from racing down the lane to tell him she'd changed her mind.

"Was that Joseph King I saw?" Joshua approached from the barn. He reached out for the hand towel hanging from her apron and wiped his hands. "If he is here to see Levi, I'm surprised he didn't stay. He will be back soon."

"He wasn't here for Levi. He came to speak with me." Katie walked toward the house and Joshua fell into step beside her.

It never ceased to amaze her that even after all these years their steps matched in stride and rhythm as if they were one.

"Whatever would he want with you? He's much too old to come courting," Joshua teased. He winked at her and she felt color flood her cheeks.

"Mind your manners, Joshua Miller, or I won't invite you in for coffee and a piece of apple pie."

Joshua paused and drew his fingers across his lips. "You draw a hard bargain, Katie Lapp, but you have a deal."

Arm brushing against arm, they climbed the porch steps.

Katie liked the way his earthy, masculine scent, laced with the fresh aroma of soap, clung to his skin and mixed with the smell of wood chips, hay and dirt that clung to his clothes. On any other man the combination might be unpleasant but not on Joshua. It was unique and masculine and made her want to breathe in the fragrance of his skin.

She liked the dimple in his cheek when he grinned

and the errant wave of hair that fell across his forehead.
She even liked the feeling of butterflies fluttering in
her stomach whenever he came close.

What was wrong with that?

Just because she had sworn off relationships with
men didn't mean she had to stop enjoying their presence.

Once Joshua settled himself at the kitchen table,
Katie placed an ample slice of pie and a hot cup of coffee in front of him. She told herself that she didn't cut
Joshua an extra large piece of pie just to try to please
him. He was a hard worker and needed the extra calo-
ries for energy, that was all.

Joshua was on his second cup of coffee and last bite
of pie when he again broached the subject of Joseph.

"I am curious, Katie. If he is not here to court you,
then what could Joseph King want with you?"

"He wants to buy my land."

Joshua looked as if he'd been taken totally off guard.
He spit his coffee back into his cup but not before some
of the hot liquid splattered on his work shirt and the re-
mainder of the brew spilled onto the table.

Katie grabbed a dish towel and hurried around the
table. She righted his mug and sopped up the spill.
Then, reacting without thought, she dabbed the towel
against the splatter on Joshua's shirt.

Within seconds she realized her mistake.

She found herself standing directly in front of him,
her hand moving from spot to spot across his chest, her
breath close enough to flutter his hair.

A sudden intimacy hung in the air between them.

She froze.

His warm brown eyes gazed at her. They flashed with an emotion that she didn't recognize, which just as quickly disappeared. His hand shot up and stilled hers. Gently he took the towel from her hands.

"I've got this," he said.

The husky, emotional timbre of his voice wrapped around her senses and filled her with questions she didn't want to answer, thoughts she wouldn't allow herself to entertain.

She realized the inappropriateness of her actions, and heat burned her throat and cheeks. Without a word, she stepped away. Snatching the mug from the table, she hurried over to the stove.

"Let me get you a fresh cup," she said, lifting the silver percolator from the burner.

"No." He stood and tossed the towel on the table. "*Danki,* but I have to get back to work."

They stared at each other for several heartbeats.

His eyes hard, intense, challenging.

Hers wary, embarrassed, denying.

Katie turned back to the stove and didn't dare move as she heard the back door slam shut.

Joshua couldn't get out of there fast enough.

He'd been shaken to his core. He wasn't sure if it had been the thought of Katie selling her land and leaving the district or if it was the overwhelming attraction he had just felt for her in that kitchen. The price of a piece of pie and a cup of coffee had been higher than he'd ever thought he'd pay.

He had almost jumped out of his skin when Katie

dabbed the hot liquid from his shirt. He had looked into those incredibly blue eyes and felt like a drowning man in a beckoning sea. Her lips had hovered mere inches from his mouth and he couldn't deny how much he had wanted to cover them with his own. Her breath had wafted across his skin and it had taken every ounce of control not to wrap his arms around her waist and pull her closer.

But he had no right.

If she knew what he had done, she would never be able to forgive him. How could she when he wasn't able to forgive himself? The Bible taught that a person must forgive another if they wished to be forgiven. When Peter asked how many times he should forgive his brother, Jesus replied "seventy times seven."

Joshua wondered what Jesus thought about forgiving oneself.

He leaned against the back wall of the barn and watched the horses grazing in the paddock. He remembered teaching Katie as a young girl how to ride bareback even though Amish girls weren't supposed to do such a thing. He remembered teaching her how to hit a ball, to bait a hook. He remembered comforting her beneath the willow tree when she'd cried because she thought Jacob did not care for her the way she cared for him.

He remembered loving her and leaving her.

He remembered his silence about so many things. He'd known about Jacob's poor choice of friends. He had known about his drinking. He'd even seen a mean streak in him once when he'd found him drunk.

But he didn't tell.

And Katie had paid the price.

The puckered scar on her wrist flashed through his mind. The memory of the wariness, hurt and fear residing in her eyes tore at his heart.

He could have saved her if he hadn't covered for Jacob…if he wasn't afraid that she might not believe him because of his declaration of love years before.

Some actions—or inactions—could result in causing others incredible pain.

Some sins—his sins—were unforgivable.

THREE

Katie sat on her porch and watched the setting sun. The sky, a myriad of bright colors mirroring the reds, oranges and yellows still visible on the trees, had hues streaked across the horizon. She drew her shawl closer around her shoulders to ward off the evening chill. It was mid-November and there had not yet been even a dusting of snow. Cold air bit her cheeks and Katie knew that wouldn't be the case much longer.

She loved twilight, a time of light and shadows, a peaceful quiet at the end of a busy day. Levi and Joshua had both returned to their homes. She was alone. A smile bowed the edges of her mouth. She felt closest to the Lord when she could enjoy the silence and talk with Him in prayer.

When her evening prayers ended, Katie placed her Bible on the table beside her and stood. She'd have to remember to take it into the house once she finished her evening chores.

She had just stepped off the last step of her porch when a car roared up the lane shooting dust and dirt in its wake.

Katie grimaced. She knew who this was. There was

no mistaking the black low-to-the ground sports car that she'd seen too much of these past two months. Mr. Henry Adams. The man drove as though no one else had a right to the road and traffic signs had no meaning. Many times she had to calm a skittish horse as he roared past her buggy on the way to town.

The car kicked up more dirt as the tires squealed to an abrupt stop.

Katie coughed as she inhaled the fine mist and waved her hand in front of her face to ward off most of it.

What a rude, arrogant man! Maybe she should say a prayer for him.

"Good evening. How are you this evening, ma'am?"

"I am quite well, Mr. Adams. Thank you for asking." She tried to keep her distaste for this man from showing on her face. "What can I do for you?"

"I was wondering if you had a chance to consider my most recent offer."

"There is nothing to consider, Mr. Adams. I've told you repeatedly that I have no intention of selling my land."

He moved closer, his smile wider but his eyes reminding her of the black eyes of a snake.

"My offer is more than generous, Mrs. Lapp. I have offered you the same amount as I have offered to your neighbor, Joseph King, even though your property is half the size."

"It does not sound like a good business decision to offer more than you believe something is worth."

He threw his head back and laughed. Unlike Joshua's laugh, which she never tired of hearing, this man's laugh sounded like nails on a blackboard and she could barely stand the sound.

"I am a kind man. I am willing to forego my small percentage of profit if it were to help a widow such as yourself."

The phoniness of his friendly demeanor soured her stomach. How could he convince anyone to do business with him? He certainly didn't seem trustworthy to her.

Another thought slowly seeped into her mind. Both Joseph King and Mr. Adams competed nonstop for her land. Just how badly did they want it? Bad enough to burn a field of crops? Bad enough to leave threatening notes on a stair post?

A sense of unease slid down her spine. It was hard to believe that Joseph King would do such a thing. But why not? Being Amish didn't make a person stop being human. Even Amish struggled with envy and greed and anger and a wide variety of other faults. And Henry Adams?

It was getting easier by the second to suspect him. He reminded her of a creepy, crawling insect, only larger and fatter. All Katie could think about was getting Mr. Adams to leave.

"I appreciate your kindness but I must turn you down. My land is not for sale."

The smile disappeared from his face.

"That remains to be seen, Mrs. Lapp."

"Please don't waste any more of your time. I will not change my mind."

"Never say *never*." The sinister, slick way the words fell from his mouth gave Katie pause. "I know you have had some misfortunes lately. I am offering you a way to ease that suffering."

A sinking feeling settled in her stomach.

Could I be right? Is this man responsible for my current troubles? He doesn't really want me dead, does he?

Katie fought the sudden urge to run and, instead, tried to sidestep around him. "If you'll excuse me, I have to attend to my chores."

He continued to block her path. "I know that more than half of your crops were destroyed in a fire. I also know you took a financial beating at the market."

Katie's heart pounded but she refrained from comment and moved past him.

"I also know, Mrs. Lapp, that someone has been leaving upsetting notes for you to find."

She gasped and came to an abrupt stop.

How can he know about the notes unless he wrote them?

"You are mistaken, sir." She offered a silent prayer that God would understand the reason for her lie and forgive her this transgression. "Where would you hear such a thing?"

"You should know that the gossip mill runs rampant in this town. Hang around the general store. You hear juicy tidbits on everyone and everything."

"Then you should consider your source, Mr. Adams. Gossip is usually just that—gossip. Now, if you'll excuse me, I must ask you to leave."

He shrugged his shoulders. "Everyone has their price, Mrs. Lapp. In time I will discover yours."

She watched as he climbed back into his fancy automobile and sped down her lane. She couldn't shake the feelings of disgust and unease that rose in her every time he came around. She sincerely hoped he would tire of her constant refusals and take his offers someplace else.

Shaking off the unsettling feelings, she went about her evening chores. She was filling the horse's troughs with fresh water when she heard a sound behind her.

"Well, there you are." She hadn't realized she'd been holding her breath until she let it go and then she laughed. "I haven't seen you for a couple of days. Did you wander off and visit your friends on other farms?"

The cat mewed loudly and, tail twitching, walked in continuous circles.

"What's the matter, huh?" Katie stooped down and gathered the gray striped cat to her chest. "Why are you so upset? No fresh mice for dinner?"

The cat wouldn't rest in her arms and resisted her attempts to pet her. Digging claws into Katie's flesh, it meowed and tried to leap out of her grasp.

Katie bent over and released the animal.

What was wrong? She'd never been scratched before.

Katie frowned and continued watching the cat pace in ever-widening circles. She couldn't imagine what was upsetting the animal. Then she heard a soft mewling coming from above her head. She looked up and had to look again to make sure her eyes weren't deceiving her. Four tiny faces hung over the loft edge, crying and pacing as they tried to get down but didn't know how.

"You're a new mama! How in the world did you get up there in the first place, mama cat? And what are you doing down here without your babies?"

Katie's gaze shot around the barn and then it dawned

on her. Several bales of hay were always stacked on top of each other just inside the back barn door to make it easier to care for the horses. The cat must have used the stacks of hay as a stepladder to the loft.

Katie frowned and that uneasy feeling came rushing back.

Someone had moved the hay.

Levi would have had no reason to move those stacks and she certainly hadn't. She cast a sweeping glance around the barn and didn't see them anywhere.

Fear niggled at the corners of her mind but she refused to let it in. She had to get up to the loft and save those kittens before they fell to their deaths. She'd worry about the missing hay later.

She glanced up once more and offered a silent prayer that God would make them stay put until she could rescue them. She figured God wouldn't mind her praying for a few kittens. They were his creations, too.

Jacob had always tended to the chores that required ladders and Levi did it after Jacob's passing. Since her husband's death in a fall, Katie had had a fear of heights, but she didn't dare wait until morning when Levi would arrive. Those kittens were hungry and they saw their mother down below. Her heart skipped a beat when she thought about what could happen if she didn't get up there in a hurry.

She'd wrap the kittens in her apron and bring them down to their mother. She hoped there weren't more than four and that they didn't run away when she approached. She had no desire to be crawling around the straw looking for frightened kittens.

The large stepladder was heavier than she realized. Dragging it across the floor, she struggled to stand it upright and drop it against the edge of the loft. She climbed three of the steps and then stopped and wrapped her arms around a rung. She felt dizzy and a little bit nauseous. A sick feeling like a mass of stone formed in the pit of her stomach. Every cell in her body wanted to get back down as quickly as possible but she knew she couldn't.

With a steely resolve, she climbed the fourth step and then another.

Her head started to spin and little spots danced in front of her eyes.

Oh, Lord! Please give me strength!

She dared to glance up. She still had several feet to go.

Maybe if I close my eyes...

Clawing the edges of the ladder, she climbed a step and then another and another. Squeezing her eyes shut, she continued to climb. Suddenly the ladder shuddered beneath her and began to rock.

It all happened so fast Katie didn't even realize the danger she was in. She was too high on the ladder to do more than flatten her body against the rails and clasp the top.

Someone below pulled the ladder away from the loft. Katie clung to the final rung with all her strength. The ladder swayed in open air and then slammed against the edge of the loft. She gasped as it swayed backward and crashed forward once again.

Katie's foot slipped from one of the rungs and she screamed.

The ladder swayed from side to side, shaking her

like a dog with a rag doll in its mouth. She hit her chin against a rung and her teeth bit into her lip. Blood lent a metallic taste.

Unable to hold on any longer, Katie found herself clawing at air. She screamed as her body slammed against the dirt floor. Pain radiated through every pore and she remained still for several seconds trying to get her bearings. She rolled over onto her knees and started to stand.

A shadow appeared in her peripheral vision. It was the shadow of a man and he held a shovel over his head.

Before she could react, that shovel connected with the back of her head. She went down, her face hitting the dirt. She groaned in agony, raised her head again and touched the back of her skull. Pulling her hand away, she stared at her bloodstained palm.

Katie didn't have time to think about who had struck her or why. She simply closed her eyes and slid into oblivion.

"Katie! Open your eyes." Joshua continued to press a towel firmly to the back of her head to stanch the bleeding but he didn't dare move her until he knew if she'd broken any bones.

His heart pounded in his chest. He hadn't believed his eyes when he'd entered the barn and seen Katie sprawled on the dirt floor. One glance at the ladder standing beside her and he knew instantly what had happened. He just hoped she hadn't been too high up when she'd fallen.

"Katie! Come on, *lieb*. Don't do this to me. Wake up."

He shook her shoulder gently. "Open your eyes, Katie. You're scaring me."

Almost as if she'd heard him, he saw her eyelids flutter. She groaned and Joshua knew she was regaining consciousness.

"That's it! Wake up."

Katie's eyelids fluttered again and again, until finally he stared into the beautiful blue eyes that he adored. He felt all his efforts to stay emotionally distant fade away. *Danki, Lord.*

But somehow a prayer of thanks didn't seem to be enough. She could have died and the pain that seized his heart was almost more than he could bear.

"Joshua?"

Her hoarse whisper was as welcome to his ears as a shout.

"*Ya,* Katie. It's me."

"The ladder… I…I was on the ladder…"

"That's not important right now. How are you hurt? Where is there pain?"

Gently he lowered her head to the floor, letting the towel act as a cushion against the dirt. Gingerly he ran his fingers down her arm, feeling for any breaks. Finding none, he stepped to her other side and repeated his movements. Nothing seemed to be broken.

"Can you raise your arms?"

His pulse beat wildly and he held his breath. This was the moment of truth. This would tell whether she'd broken her back or her neck or injured her spine.

A sense of relief washed over him when she lifted her arms.

"Katie, can you move your feet back and forth?"

Seconds ticked by and Joshua thought he might never draw a breath again when she didn't move.

"Katie? Lift one of your legs, please."

It seemed to take her another moment to comprehend what he asked but elation raced through his every pore when she not only pumped her feet but also moved both legs. Pulling up her knees, she tried to sit up.

"Whoa! Where do you think you're going?" Joshua gently forced her shoulders back down. "You've just had a nasty spill. Give yourself a minute or two before you try to get up and walk."

Katie groaned again and lifted a hand toward her head. Joshua caught it in midair. "I know. Your head must hurt. I'll get you inside and tend to it just as soon as I'm sure I won't make things worse by moving you."

He leaned in closer and stared into Katie's eyes. He hoped she wouldn't see the tears he fought to hold at bay.

"You scared me. When I came in and found you on the floor, lying perfectly still, bleeding…" He reached down and brushed a loose tendril of hair from her cheek. The silky smoothness of her skin against his fingertips sent chills down his spine. To think that he'd almost lost her. He gritted his teeth and refused to let his emotions rule the moment.

"I should have known better. It takes more than a little spill from a ladder to stop Katie Lapp." He slid his arms beneath her. "Let's try to sit up. I'll help you." He supported her shoulders as she rose to a sitting position.

She caught her breath and clasped her head with both hands.

"What happened?" she whispered.

"I was hoping you could tell me. What were you doing climbing that ladder? There's no reason for you to be in the loft."

"Kittens. I was bringing them down to their mother."

"What?" Joshua strained his neck to look up and then glanced back at her. "Well, if the mother cat was down here, she must have clawed her way back up, because she's lying there nursing her brood without a care in the world. Unlike you, I'm afraid."

He tilted her chin to the side to get a better look at the back of her head.

"I'm surprised you fell from the ladder. The Katie I knew as a kid could hold her weight on a vine and swing out over the pond without falling." He chuckled at the memory.

"I wasn't afraid of heights when I was younger. I seem to be now." She offered a timid smile. "Besides, I didn't fall. Someone threw me off."

The laughter died in his throat. "Someone did this to you on purpose? Who would do such a thing?"

"I don't know," Katie replied. "I was too busy holding on for dear life to look below and see who it was."

"Are you sure, Katie? Maybe the ladder tipped beneath your weight."

"Then why is the ladder still standing? *Ya,* I'm sure. I don't know who and I don't know why, but I am absolutely sure of what happened."

"Enough is enough. I do not care what Levi thinks. It is time we go to the police." He slid one arm beneath her legs, the other behind her back and lifted her into his arms.

"What are you doing, Joshua? Put me down. I can walk."

"I'm not letting you walk anywhere until I tend to that head wound and make sure that you are steady on your feet." He held her tightly in his arms. She felt so tiny and light and fragile, a far cry from the little spitfire that stood her ground the first day he'd challenged her in the barn, the one who wasn't scared of confrontation from anyone.

"Grab the oil lamp." He paused just long enough for her to do as he asked. The lamp lit their way as he walked across the darkened yard.

Katie's *kapp* brushed against his chin and he could smell the fresh fragrance of her hair mixed with the coppery scent of her blood.

He thought he was going to choke on his anger. This was no longer just a word scribbled on paper. This was sinister, evil. Someone had done this to Katie on purpose. She could have been killed.

His mind refused to even entertain the thought of a world without Katie in it.

He would find out who did this to her. He only hoped he'd be able to do it before anything worse happened to Katie.

Even through his concern, he realized that she wasn't objecting or demanding that she walk to the house on her own. Was that because she was finally letting down her guard and allowing him to help her? Or was it because her head injury was more serious than he'd thought?

For a brief instant he didn't care about the reason. It

felt so good to cradle her in his arms, to protect her— even if it was just for a moment, just for this one reason.

He knew he was losing touch with the emotional distance he'd demanded of himself.

He couldn't let that happen.

It wouldn't be good for either one of them.

Katie made it quite clear she didn't want to get involved in a relationship with any man. He couldn't bear opening his heart and having her reject it again.

No. He had to get his emotions under control and retain his distance. But what would it hurt to enjoy the closeness for one more moment? He cradled her just a little bit closer, his arms and his heart aching at the thought of having to let her go.

Suddenly a thought popped into his head and dread filled his mind.

Had Katie been conscious when he'd spoken to her in the barn?

Had she heard him call her *lieb?*

She had had a bad fall and had been knocked senseless. Even if she had heard his words, she would have dismissed them as nothing more than confusion caused by her head injury.

Joshua didn't want to think about any other possibility. His mind raced as he tried to remember those first few moments in the barn and then he relaxed. He was certain everything would be fine.

There was no way that Katie could have heard him call her "love."

FOUR

When they reached the porch, Joshua snatched the lantern handle in his fingers, being careful not to loosen the hold he had on Katie's legs. At the door, he had her reach down and turn the knob. Kicking it open the rest of the way, he paused in the doorway. The illuminated sight inside made his blood run cold.

He placed the lamp on the nearest porch table before putting Katie in the closest chair. Not wasting another second, he crossed the floor and beat the metal triangle hanging from the eaves. The clanging sound filled the night air.

"Joshua!" She covered her ears with her hands. "What are you doing?"

She steadied herself on the edges of the chairs and planters but she made her way to him. "Stop, Joshua. What are you doing? Everyone will come."

"*Ya,* Katie. That's what I want," he said, ignoring her hand and continuing to hit the metal form.

"But why? I don't understand."

"Look inside but do not go in. Stay on the porch with me until help comes."

Katie moved toward the door. He saw her pick up

the lantern and hold it high against the darkness inside. Within seconds she lowered her arm and leaned heavily against the doorjamb. Joshua could see the color drain from her face.

He knew what she saw.

Someone had ransacked the house. Broken pieces of furniture were strewn across the floor. Books ripped. Pillows emptied. A two-foot-high word clung to the wall over the fireplace— *Leave!*

Why was this happening to her? Joshua wondered. Someone had burned her fields, sent her threatening notes, pushed her off a ladder and now this…

Katie, her clothes splattered with her own blood, met Joshua's gaze. He could see the terror in her eyes. But he also saw the subtle squaring of her shoulders.

There she was! The Katie he knew. The Katie who wouldn't run, who would find the strength to get through anything God sent her way.

She looked away and bowed her head. He saw the slight movement of her lips and knew this was exactly what she needed.

Katie was praying.

The flashing strobe lights of the police cruiser and the red lights of the ambulance danced in circles across the porch.

One of the paramedics cleaned and bandaged Katie's head wound. "You're lucky," he said, squatting down to close his bag. "You could have been seriously hurt. I can't find anything more than a few bumps and bruises," he continued, "but with a head wound, we should take you to the hospital for a more thorough checkup."

"That will not be necessary," Katie said. "The good Lord protected me. I have no need to go anywhere but inside my own home. *Danki.*" She gave him a dismissive smile.

The man acknowledged her words with a nod and carried his bag back to his rig.

"How could such a terrible thing be happening here?" Amos Fischer, bishop of their small district, asked. "We are a quiet, peaceful community."

"Evil happens everywhere, Amos, even in God's country," Joseph King replied.

Several other neighbors, gathered in small groups on her porch and at the base of the steps, agreed as they watched the paramedics and the police finish their work.

"How are you feeling, Katie? Did you see who did this to you?" Levi sat down beside her. "I am grateful to Joshua for finding you when he did. I hate to think what could have happened if you had lain there all night with a bleeding head wound."

Levi looked up at Joshua, who stood behind Katie and had been silent this whole time. "Why were you here at such a late hour, Joshua?"

"I was returning home later than planned from a job I had done for Eli. I could see the barn lights from the road but there were no lights in the house. I found it strange that Katie would be in the barn at such an hour and I came to see if everything was all right. I am glad that I did."

A murmur of agreement moved through the crowd.

"You must have fallen on your head to receive such an injury," Levi said. "I checked the barn. The ladder was still standing and there was nothing on the floor for you to hit your head on."

"She didn't hit the floor. Someone hit her from behind."

Everyone turned toward the sheriff as he walked across the yard and joined the group at the edge of the porch.

"I believe this could put a healthy dent in anyone's head. I found it tossed in the back of one of the horse's stalls." The sheriff held up a shovel covered in dried blood.

Esther, Amos Fischer's wife, gasped. "Come with me, child. You shouldn't have to see this. Let me get you inside. I'll make you a hot cup of tea while you get ready for bed."

Katie rose. She was grateful for the help. Grateful not to have to look at the shovel. Grateful not to think about who hated her so much that they swung a shovel to the back of her head.

Her eyes sought out Joshua. He leaned against the porch wall, arms crossed, listening and not saying much.

But that was the Joshua that Katie remembered. Always standing in the background. Quiet. Yet ever present.

His dark eyes stared intently at her.

"*Danki* for helping me," she whispered.

Joshua nodded. *Always, Katie,* he mouthed back.

Katie woke hearing voices coming from downstairs. She went down to investigate. When she reached the bottom of the steps, she could see several women from the district cooking in the kitchen. Others were cleaning the remnants of the mess from the night before.

Esther looked up from sweeping broken glass from the living room floor. "*Guder mariye,* Katie. Are you sure you should be up?"

Katie smiled. "*Ya.* A little headache and a couple of bumps and bruises. Nothing to worry about." She noted that someone had already scrubbed away the word that the intruder had scrawled over the fireplace. What could be salvaged of the furniture was back in place, and the delicious smell of bacon and eggs mingled with those of casseroles the women had prepared for dinner. The enticing scent wafted from the kitchen and her stomach growled.

"I appreciate everyone's efforts." Katie smiled at the women. *"Danki."*

"This is what we do," Esther said. She wrapped her arm around Katie's waist and continued talking as she led her into the kitchen. "We take care of our own."

Several *ya*s came from the other women.

Katie enjoyed the breakfast. She thanked the women for the two casseroles fresh from the oven. She was grateful for their help but right now she just wanted everyone to leave. Her physical wounds might not be severe but her emotional wounds were taking their toll.

She had barely slept last night. She had no idea why someone wanted her to leave this district, to leave her home, but suddenly Katie found herself giving serious thought to the suggestion. She had some distant cousins on her mother's side living in an Ohio district. Maybe she could go there.

Probably seeing her fatigue, the women wished Katie well and took their leave.

Esther, the only one to remain behind, invited Katie to sit down at the table, then turned to retrieve two cups from the cupboard.

"Katie!"

At the sound of her name, she turned to see Levi, obviously agitated about something, tramp through the living room and into the kitchen.

"Did you ask these men to come?" he queried, waving his hat toward the window.

"What men? I don't know what you are talking about, Levi."

She made her way to the window. One glance outside and she felt a wave of anger. Joseph King and Mr. Adams were having an animated conversation. "No, Levi. I did not ask these men to come. Could you please ask them to leave?"

"Gladly." Levi shoved his hat back onto his head and stomped out the door.

Katie watched for a moment, sighed heavily and returned to the table. She looked down at the cup Esther set in front of her.

"Chocolate, Esther? This early in the morning?" She smiled at the older woman.

"It is never too early for chocolate, child." Esther patted the seat beside her. "Come. Sit. Levi will handle whatever the problem is outside."

Katie didn't need a second invitation. She sipped her drink and then ran her tongue over the chocolate foam ringing her lips. Both women laughed.

"See," Esther said. "Chocolate can make all your problems disappear."

"I wish it was that easy."

Esther gave her a puzzled glance.

Katie took another sip of her drink before Esther asked, "And which man is going to buy your land?"

She looked up in surprise.

"This is a small community. You know that. Besides, Mr. Adams has been approaching all of us with offers for our land. Joseph surprises me but I suppose I shouldn't be surprised. Your property touches his. It makes perfect sense that he would rather expand than share a border with an Englischer."

"What makes you think that I'm going to sell? Do you, too, want me to go?" Katie knew her tone was defensive and held a bristled edge, but she couldn't help it. She felt alone and unwelcome in her own community, and it hurt.

Esther simply smiled and placed a hand on top of hers. "You know better than that, child. None of us want you to leave. But what choice do you have?" She patted her hand. "It has been a year and a half since Jacob's death, *ya?* You have turned down every man who has tried to come courting. You cannot do this work all on your own."

"I am not doing it alone. Levi helps."

"You and Levi have done a fine job trying to keep the farm running. But, Katie, Levi has his own farm that he has been tending. Everyone can see it has taken a toll on him. He won't be able to help you forever, even if you are family."

Tears burned the back of Katie's eyes. "And if I choose to stay?"

Esther shrugged then picked up her mug and took a sip. "That is surely your choice." She gestured with her hand toward the fireplace easily visible from the kitchen. "But someone wants you to leave. It might be wise for you to take the money and go while you still can. Get a fresh start. Start a new life."

Katie caught Esther's eyes. "Why is someone doing this to me? Who do you think it is?"

"It must be the Englischer. I'm not particularly fond of Joseph King, but he is one of us and I cannot believe that greed would make him cross that line. But no matter who it is, I do not believe they intend to stop." Esther's eyes glistened with unshed tears. "I don't want to see anything happen to you."

Katie clasped the older woman's hands. "*Danki*, Esther. You are right. I must make a decision soon on what to do with my life." She sighed heavily. "I'll talk with Levi and see what he would advise."

"*Gut.* It is necessary to talk with family when you have to make such an important decision." She pointed her index finger toward the ceiling. "But it is best to talk to God. Let Him direct your path."

Esther took a last sip of her chocolate. A twinkle appeared in her eyes. "Of course, you would not have to sell your land if you married again. Joshua Miller, perhaps?"

Katie gasped. "Joshua? Whatever makes you say such a thing? Joshua is a childhood friend."

"*Ya.*" Esther nodded. "But he is not a child anymore. He is a grown man and from what my eyes can see he is dependable, hardworking and handsome. That cannot hurt, *ya*?"

The memory of Joshua's voice flooded back.

Katie! Come on, lieb. *Don't do this to me. Wake up.*

Esther stood and placed a hand gently on Katie's shoulder. "It seems you have many things to pray about, child. I will leave you to it."

Katie followed Esther onto the porch and waved at the buggy as she pulled away.

Levi approached from the barn. "I told both men to leave and not to come back again."

"*Danki* for handling that for me, Levi." Katie sat down. "Could you spare me a moment, please?"

Levi sat down opposite her. "What is it? Do you feel ill? Do you wish for me to take you to a doctor?"

"No." She waved her hand. "I'm fine. Just a small headache. It will go away."

"What, then?" Levi asked.

"I need your council."

Levi waited silently.

"You are Jacob's brother and you have done a wonderful job helping me after his death…."

"That is my job. The Bible says when a brother dies then the oldest should step up and take his place. I am the only brother Jacob had. It is my duty to provide for his widow."

Katie felt a twinge of guilt. Levi tended his own farm and then did his best to run hers, as well. Lately he had started hiring people when the workload became more than he could handle. People like Joshua.

Her gaze wandered to the open barn door and Katie

couldn't help but wonder if Joshua had arrived and might be already working inside.

Levi frowned when he saw the direction of Katie's gaze. "I do not have time to waste." He stood. "Do you have something you wish to ask me or not?"

Katie blushed when she realized Levi knew where her eyes—and her mind—had wandered.

"I have two considerable monetary offers on the farm, Levi. Enough money that I could leave this place and never have another financial worry."

Levi looked as if she'd slapped him. "Do not tell me that you are thinking of selling? Why, Katie? Haven't I been running things to your satisfaction? Haven't I been working hard enough?"

She jumped to her feet and put her hand on his forearm. "Levi, you have done a wonderful job. I don't know what I would have done without you. But…" Her words trailed away.

"If you want to leave, then leave. I will not try to stop you. If you need money to leave, then I will give you money." His eyes hardened. "But this is Lapp land. It does not belong to Joseph King and it certainly does not belong to an Englischer."

He turned, bolted down the steps and disappeared behind the barn.

"That didn't go well."

Katie jumped and turned toward the sound of the voice. "Where did you come from? I thought you'd be working in the barn."

Joshua hopped over the porch railing on the far side. "My work in the barn is finished. I am beginning my repairs on the house."

"You've got to stop sneaking up on me. You've scared me twice now," she scolded.

Joshua laughed. "You never used to be afraid of me."

"That's because you never sneaked up on me. I always knew you were nearby."

"How so?"

"Don't you remember?" Katie teased. "I nicknamed you The Shadow because you always seemed to be right behind me."

"And now?" Joshua stepped closer.

She could feel his breath on her face and smell the minty tang. She stared at his lips and couldn't help but wonder what those lips would feel like pressed against her own.

"Are you going to kiss me?" she whispered and then wished the words had not escaped her lips.

His expression darkened. "You are Jacob's widow. I have no right to kiss you…now or ever."

Katie colored. "I was simply teasing you, Joshua. You are standing so close and you always were so shy…." Her voice trailed off as they stared at each other.

"Make no mistake. I am not that shy teenager anymore, Katie." The huskiness in his voice held a deeper meaning. The intensity of his stare challenged her.

Joshua *wanted* to kiss her.

She could see it in his eyes. She could sense it in his tense body language.

And she wanted to kiss him back.

The thought scared her to death.

Both of them stepped away almost simultaneously.

What was happening to her? She couldn't afford to let another man into her life or her heart. She refused to forfeit control over her wants and needs and become a submissive wife again. She'd lived in silence through a bad marriage, a horribly abusive marriage. She'd kept Jacob's secret. But at what cost to herself?

No, never again.

She'd never trust another man. She'd never relinquish control. Never.

But her heart thundered in her chest when her eyes locked with Joshua's. Her stomach clenched and her pulse raced like wild horses.

She could trust Joshua, couldn't she?

Katie took another step back. Once upon a time she had thought she could trust Jacob.

"I…I have to go." She backed toward the door. "I…I have to tend to things on the stove."

Katie turned and practically ran inside.

FIVE

Enjoying the twilight—and the silence—Katie closed her eyes, leaned her head back and tried to ignore the familiar tightening in her chest. Autumn and spring were the worst times. So many allergens triggered her asthma during these seasons that she'd lost count of the list of things the doctor had warned her to avoid.

Of course, stress headed the top of the list and she had to admit she was on stress overload these days.

She practiced taking long, deep breaths through her nose and then released the air slowly through pursed lips.

Diaphragmatic breathing, the doctor had called it.

She didn't care what he called it. She only knew that sometimes it helped to ease an impending attack—that and a puff on the inhaler she carried with her at all times.

This time the breathing wasn't helping. She still felt as if a giant fist was inside her chest and squeezing the air right out of her.

She withdrew the inhaler and drew a puff into her mouth. She hated depending on medicine. She hated showing any sign of weakness at all. She was finished being weak.

Four nights had passed since the incident in the barn. Three nights of being almost constantly under Levi's and Joshua's watch. At first, it had annoyed her. She was perfectly capable of taking care of herself. But both men seemed determined to make sure nothing and no one would hurt her again. Once she got past her pride, she was grateful for the attention and the company.

The men worked out a schedule between them. Tonight, guard duty fell to Joshua. A smile touched her lips. If Levi had any idea how dangerous her feelings were every time she was around Joshua, he would have probably provided her with a guard dog instead.

"It's good to see you smile again."

This time she didn't startle. Although she hadn't heard him approach, she was becoming accustomed to his presence. During the day, when she could hear him hammering away on the roof, she knew it wouldn't be long before the hammering would cease and he'd steal a moment to check on her before returning to his work.

It probably should have upset her—that feeling of always being spied on, the inference that she needed a man around and couldn't cope on her own.

But it didn't.

It made her feel safe. Protected.

She opened her eyes.

Joshua stood in the shadows but she hadn't had to hear his voice to know it was him. Just one glance his way would have told her. Even in shadows she knew his height, the breadth of his shoulders, the way his energy filled a room—or a porch—with his presence.

"Hello, Joshua. I didn't hear you approach."

He stepped into the yellow glow of the lantern. "Yet you didn't jump. We're making progress."

She smiled widely. She had to admit she enjoyed watching him work and particularly enjoyed when he sat with her for a while.

Almost as if he could read her mind, Joshua pulled over a chair. They sat in companionable silence for a long time, enjoying the twilight, lost in their own thoughts, yet Katie was certain their thoughts were never far from each other. There was a tension between them. An awareness that filled the air with electricity.

She could feel his eyes watching her now.

"Are you hungry? Can I fix you something to eat?" she asked.

"No." He laughed. "I'm still full from the lunch you made me. If I continue to eat your good cooking, I am going to be too fat to climb up onto the roof."

Her eyes wandered to his flat stomach. She couldn't imagine how even one pound of flesh would appear to be anything on him but solid muscle.

For some reason, he seemed reluctant to leave this evening. More so than on other nights. She could tell he had something on his mind. Something that hid behind his eyes and yet wanted to pour out.

She shot him a questioning look but remained quiet. He'd talk when he was ready. The Joshua she remembered didn't say much, but when he did his words held their own power and importance.

"Are you finished with the roof?" she asked, giving him the time he needed to say whatever it was that troubled him.

"*Ya,* it is done."

She smiled. "*Gut.* What does Levi have you working on next?"

"Nothing. I am finished. It is time for me to go."

Her eyes flew to his face. She knew she couldn't hide her disappointment. Was that what he was finding so difficult to say?

"I'm sorry to hear that, Joshua. I was getting used to having to feed you."

She smiled as she spoke the teasing words but she didn't feel lighthearted. Her heart felt heavy and sad.

"I am still your neighbor, Katie. I intend to come by and see if you need anything."

"That would be nice."

Inane words, meaning nothing but saying everything. He was telling her he would never be far away. She was telling him she wanted him near. Yet their actual words told one another nothing of importance at all.

"Katie."

The seriousness of his tone caught her attention.

"I've wanted to ask you…about Jacob."

Heat flooded her cheeks and she lowered her eyes. She'd thought she'd put the anger behind her months ago. She'd thought she could hear his name and not think the things she did or feel the way she did.

She was wrong.

She didn't know if she was ready to talk about Jacob to anyone. She didn't know if she ever could. She shrugged nonchalantly as if Joshua's words carried no weight. "What is there to say? Jacob is dead."

Joshua leaned closer but refrained from touching her. "How did he die?"

"You know how he died. He fell during a barn raising and broke his neck." Anger flashed in her eyes when she looked at him. Her tone challenged him. "You didn't come back for the funeral but I am sure you were told of his death. Your cousin's district wasn't that far away."

Empathy and something else, compassion, perhaps, shone in his gaze.

She shifted uncomfortably. "Why do you want to know about his death now? It happened over a year ago."

"*Ya,* it did." He sighed heavily. "But you haven't re-married."

"That's none of your concern, Joshua Miller." She tapped her foot in a nervous rhythm against the porch floor. Her stress level rose.

"No, you're right. It's not." He tilted her chin toward him. "But I'm asking just the same. Why haven't you been courting? It would solve your land problem."

She jumped to her feet. "Is that what you think, Joshua Miller? That poor Katie Lapp needs a man to save her? Well, I don't. I am a strong, independent woman who can fend for herself. I can make my own decisions. I don't need a man to tell me what to do. And especially not you!"

Joshua stood and clasped her forearms in his hands.

Immediately, she pushed at him and tried to pull from his grasp. "Take your hands off me!" She pulled harder. "Let me go!"

He released his hold. His stunned expression almost brought her to tears.

She tried to take a breath and almost panicked when one didn't come. She gasped and then gasped again.

"Katie!" He put his hands on her again but this time with a gentleness that touched her heart. "It's your asthma, isn't it?" He guided her into the rocking chair. "I'd forgotten. You used to have attacks quite often when we were kids."

She pulled the inhaler out of her pouch and again drew the medication into her lungs.

Joshua squatted in front of her, waiting, watching.

When her breathing returned to a normal rhythm, Joshua locked his gaze with hers.

"Talk to me, Katie." His voice was soft and tender. "What happened to you in the years I've been gone?"

Tears burned the back of her eyes but she refused to shed even one. She couldn't answer him. She couldn't speak at all. Her pain cut too deep.

Slowly, so gently and so softly it took her breath away, he kissed her. It wasn't the kiss that did her in. It was the kindness, the tenderness, the empathy she felt in it, and the floodgates opened. She sobbed and, try as she might, she couldn't stop. It was as though years of pent-up tears finally broke through the impenetrable wall she'd built around her heart.

Joshua pulled her down onto the floor with him. Cradling her in his arms. Rocking her with his body. Comforting her with his words.

After what seemed an eternity, she stopped crying and he looked deeply into her eyes.

"Talk to me, *lieb*. Tell me what is wrong. Is it about Jacob?"

Katie nodded.

"Do you miss him that much? Even after all this time?"

Her sadness melted into anger as volatile as molten lava. "Miss him? I hated him!" Immediately her hands flew to her lips. She wished she could call back her words but, of course, she couldn't.

Joshua sat back on his legs and stared at her. "You can't mean that!"

She lowered her eyes, unable to meet his gaze. "God forgive me but it's true."

"Why, Katie?" He couldn't hide his shock or keep the mild censure from his voice. "What would make you say such a thing about Jacob?"

"Jacob wasn't Jacob. He wasn't the boy we grew up with. He wasn't the teenager I loved. He was a monster."

Seconds of silence beat between them.

Joshua reached out and took her hand. "Tell me."

Katie wanted to tell him. She needed to tell him. She'd never spoken of those days. Not even to God. She'd been too angry, too hurt…too scared that somehow it had all been her fault and she couldn't face it.

But she looked into Joshua's eyes and saw no censure there. Only compassion.

"Jacob drank alcohol and he became a different person when he did." Her eyes implored him to believe her. "I never would have married him if I had known he was bringing this sickness into our marriage."

Her fingers couldn't find rest. They pulled at the edges of her apron, fiddled with the string of her *kapp*.

"Why didn't you go to the elders?"

"Because it was Jacob." The saddest of smiles pulled at the corners of her mouth. "At first, he would cry and beg for my forgiveness. He'd promise to never do it again. For months, he would keep his word…and they'd be good months. He would bring me wildflowers from the fields. He would hold my hand and take long walks with me by the pond. We would talk of our future, of the family we both wanted. Then he would drink again. Oh, he would apologize—again. He'd stop for a while until I started to believe that this time he was free of that poison. But over time a pattern formed. I knew Jacob wouldn't stop…couldn't stop."

"When you knew he couldn't stop, why didn't you tell the elders then?"

She lowered her head and all the bravado she had shown Joshua since he'd returned was gone, all the anger emptied. All that was left was pain and self-blame.

"I was afraid of him."

"Of Jacob?" Joshua was incredulous. "How could anyone be afraid of Jacob? I would never have believed he'd raise his hand to any woman and certainly not to you."

She looked accusingly at him and he realized instantly that he'd said the wrong thing, reacted the wrong way.

"I'm sorry," he whispered. "I had no right to judge." He ran the tips of his fingers ever so gently down her cheek. "I knew Jacob as a boy. I didn't know him as a man."

"The alcohol made him different." Her voice sounded listless and empty. "He wasn't the Jacob I knew. He wasn't the Jacob anybody knew." She put out her hand and held her wrist face up. "He hurt me. He'd take delight in proving his strength, his power over me."

Joshua blanched when his gaze fell to the scars on her wrist. Although he'd seen them before, a fresh wave of rage washed over him. He clasped her wrist in his hand. "He did this to you?" He'd heard the women gossiping in the corner of the general store that things weren't right between them but he assumed it was the drinking. He never believed his friend could grow up into this kind of man.

"He promised he would do much worse than this if I ever spoke of his drinking to anyone…so I didn't. After he died, I promised myself that I would never again be a victim. That I would never again let a man control my life."

"I'm sorry, Katie. I'm so sorry." He slid his fingers across her rippled scars.

She shrugged. "You have no reason to apologize."

All of it made sense now. The hostility he sensed in her from that very first day in the barn. The edginess. The wariness in her eyes. The dullness in eyes that used to be bright. The bravado and false sense of independence. Her difficulty accepting help from anyone except Levi.

Joshua rubbed a hand over his face. To get her to go to the police that very first day, he'd grabbed her hand and pulled her behind him. She'd erupted in anger, a side of her he had never seen before. Now he understood. He must have seemed like just another bully trying to force her to do something she hadn't wanted to do. He understood it all—and it made him physically ill.

Please, God. Help me. How will she ever forgive me? Especially now.

How can I ever forgive myself?

Everything in him wanted to slink off into the cover of darkness.

But he couldn't.

No matter how she reacted—with anger, with a slap, with a vow to never speak to him again—she deserved to know the truth.

Joshua stood. He extended his hand and helped her to her feet.

"I cannot apologize enough, Katie. My heart breaks for what you have gone through."

Katie smiled up at him, such a sweet, endearing smile. She cupped the side of his face with her hand.

"You have nothing to apologize for, Joshua. You have been a good friend." Her smile widened. "It is because of you that I have the courage to speak of these things to someone. It has helped me more than you know." She stood on tiptoe and kissed his cheek. *"Danki."*

He clasped her forearms and gently moved her away. He knew from the expression on her face that she believed he couldn't accept the things she'd said. He knew he had to set things right—now—no matter what the cost.

"I have done a horrible thing."

Katie pulled her shawl tighter around her body. "I don't understand." Her confusion and perhaps a touch of fear appeared on her face. "What have you done but listen to me? Help me? Be the best friend that I have missed all these years?"

Her tears…and smiles…and questions were ripping his heart out.

"I have not been the friend to you that I should have

been. I should have been here for you. I should have stopped Jacob."

Katie laughed mirthlessly. "That's nonsense, Joshua. How could you have stopped Jacob? You didn't know. Nobody knew. He hid it well."

Bile rose in his throat and at that moment he hated himself more than she ever could.

"I knew."

He watched her smile slip away. Doubt filled her eyes only to quickly fade into shock and finally realization.

"You knew?" she whispered in disbelief.

He nodded.

"I don't understand. What did you know? When did you know?" She clasped her hand to her chest and seemed to be holding her breath while she waited for his answer.

"I knew he drank, shortly after you were married. I knew right before I left for my cousin's."

Her eyes searched the ground as if she'd find answers in the dirt, answers she'd been unable to draw from him.

When she lifted her eyes, the sense of betrayal he saw in them was almost more than he could bear. "I can't believe you didn't warn me."

When she spoke again, her voice was calm, controlled. "How did you find out?"

"One night I found him by the side of the road. I helped him into my buggy and then I realized that he was drunk. He told me it was the first and only time. He had met up with some Englisch friends that he had hung out with during *rumspringa*. Foolishly he had gone with them to a local bar. Jacob assured me that he would never do it again. He told me that he could never disrespect you or your marriage. He begged me to keep silent and I did."

Katie paced in a small circle. She seemed to be trying to process this new information. "Do you have any idea what your silence cost me?" Absently she rubbed her wrists. "He hurt me, Joshua. He forced his will on me so many times. He grew to take pleasure in knowing I was powerless against him. And the worst of it?" Tears shimmered in her eyes. "He made me believe I was a terrible wife. He told me over and over that his drinking was my fault."

Joshua could not speak. What could he possibly say? The knowledge that his silence had caused her such pain felt as if someone had stabbed him in the heart.

"Why did you leave Hope's Creek? Why didn't you stay and see if Jacob could keep his word?"

"I believed him, Katie. Do you think if I knew that it was more than once, if I thought for even one moment that he was lying to me, that I would have kept silent no matter how much he begged? He was my friend. But you…you were so much more."

Katie just stood and stared at him.

He didn't know what bothered him most, that she didn't yell at him, slap him or tell him to get out of her life—or if it was the sadness and the disappointment he saw in her eyes.

"Tell me the truth, Joshua. Why did you leave? You were a farmer. I never heard you express a desire to work with wood. Not once in all the years I've known you. No one understood why you chose to leave so abruptly." She pinned him with her gaze. "Tell me now. I want to know."

And there it was—the crux of the matter.

"Because I loved you." He didn't know how he found the strength to force the words out of his mouth but she deserved to know the truth, all of it. He released a heavy sigh. "I loved you and you were married to my best friend." He threw his hands up in surrender. "How could I possibly stay?"

Tears streamed down Katie's face. "Oh, Joshua, what have you done?"

SIX

Joshua stepped off the porch into the darkness. He didn't know what he'd expected. What should he expect when he'd just told the love of his life that he'd kept silent about her husband's drinking and that silence had cost her emotional pain and physical abuse for years? How could he ever look her in the eyes again?

He walked around the perimeter of her house making sure it was secure. Although he rattled windows and twisted doorknobs, he could think of nothing but the look on Katie's face just before she turned and went into the house.

She'd never forgive him.

He didn't deserve to be forgiven.

Joshua stepped into the barn. He checked every stall. He climbed the ladder and peered into the loft.

No one.

Nothing.

Katie was locked in and safe for the night.

Joshua, feeling the weight of the world on his shoulders, began the trek home. As he walked he relived the events of the evening. He could hear her voice in his mind as clearly as if she stood right beside him. His mind replayed every word. His memory burned images in his brain.

Katie smiling up at him.

Katie cupping his face.

Katie leaning into his kiss and kissing him back.

Katie crying and looking totally betrayed just moments before she walked inside the house and closed the door.

Dear heavenly Father, forgive me. Katie suffered for years because I stayed silent. How am I going to live with that?

Joshua was halfway home when he saw Levi's buggy coming his way. He sidestepped just as Levi pulled to a stop beside him.

"I thought you'd still be at Katie's."

"I made sure that no one is lurking around and that everything is locked up tight. She'll be safe until morning."

Levi nodded. "I certainly hope so. This is all becoming too much to handle. I am going to offer Katie money for the farm. I can't afford to give her what Adams and King are offering. But I believe out of respect for all the hard work that I have done, she will sell the land to me and keep it in the Lapp family where it belongs."

The thought of Katie leaving Hope's Creek permanently was more painful than the thought that she'd never speak to him again. At least if she stayed here he would still be able to see her…and he could hope that things might change. He'd stopped believing in forgiveness but he still hoped for miracles.

"I don't think tonight is a good time to broach the subject, Levi."

"That was not my intention. I will bring up the subject tomorrow at breakfast. So many things have been happening to her lately that I am sure she is more than ready to leave."

Joshua's heart sank because he believed it, too.

"Climb in. I will turn around and take you home. It will not take me more than a few minutes out of my way."

Joshua shook his head. "*Danki,* but no. I wish to walk. I need to clear my head and walking does that for me."

"As you wish." Levi said, "I will settle my account with you tomorrow."

Joshua shrugged. "No hurry."

"I am a man who pays his debts. You did good work, Joshua. I am grateful."

Joshua acknowledged the compliment with a nod. The Amish didn't waste words on compliments. It could cause the recipient to be prideful. So why did Levi do so now?

"Since the house has been repaired and the stalls finished, there will be no need for you to come over anymore." Levi smiled but there was no warmth in his eyes. If Joshua didn't know better, he would have thought it a veiled threat.

Again, his mind went to Katie. "You're right, Levi. There will be no reason for me to come out to the farm again."

"*Gut.* Then I will be certain to stop by your house in the morning and settle our account." With a nod and a crack of his whip, Levi urged his horse on.

Fifteen minutes later, Joshua reached the lane leading to home. He'd never felt this dejected or hopeless. He'd lost Katie once because he'd been too much of a coward to tell her what was on his mind. How ironic that he'd lost her again because this time he did.

Katie sat in her bedroom in the dark and stared out the window. She didn't light her oil lamp. She wanted to just sit quietly and gaze at the stars. She didn't want to think, didn't want to feel. She just wanted to be.

The full moon cast a glow over the yard below. A movement in the shadows caught her eye. She stared hard and waited for it to move again.

The mother cat appeared out of the shadows. She was on the prowl for tonight's dinner. Katie smiled humorlessly. *And life goes on.*

She almost got up to go to bed when a movement caught her eye, a second shadow, this one larger and more cumbersome. She squinted her eyes to focus and stared harder at the shadows by the barn.

Was someone down there?

Her heart pounded. She didn't dare breathe as she stared at the spot where she thought she'd seen movement.

The shadow moved. Someone definitely moved in the darkness. Thankful for a full moon, she prayed that the person would step out of the shadows just long enough for her to see who it was.

But it didn't happen.

The person moved stealthily, carefully, hanging back in the gloom, hiding in the murkiness.

From the size of the moving mass, she felt fairly certain that her intruder was a man.

A man who was creeping into her barn!

Katie didn't know what to do. She wanted to discover who it was that tormented her. She wanted to sneak downstairs, tiptoe out to the barn and peek inside at the intruder. Once she knew who it was, she'd tell the sheriff and the elders and the whole world if need be just to be able to expose the culprit once and for all.

That was what she wanted to do.

But she wasn't stupid.

She knew she was alone in the house. She had no weapon even though she wouldn't use one if she did. Levi wouldn't be here until morning and Joshua... Joshua would probably never come out here again.

So she continued to sit in the darkness and stared at the barn door. Whoever went in had to come out. Maybe she'd see the culprit then.

Katie found that time moved exceedingly slow when a person had to wait. Seconds became minutes and every minute felt like a lifetime.

What was the person doing in the barn? Was he stealing her horses or her tack and farm equipment? Maybe this time the culprit would leave her a note lying on a bale of hay.

She was so nervous she thought she was going to jump out of her skin.

Maybe she should go downstairs. She might get a better look at who it was if she crept out onto the porch. This man wasn't the only person who could hide in the shadows.

But what if he came out of the barn while she was going downstairs? She wouldn't know and she'd lose her only opportunity to identify her tormentor.

She waited another five minutes, then ten.

Unable to stand it, she sprang to her feet. She'd take her chances. She was going to hide on the porch. She couldn't just sit here and do nothing.

Before she could move, she saw it.

She wasn't sure at first. It was just the tiniest light and for a moment Katie thought the foolish man had actually taken a chance and lit a lantern.

But the light grew…and spread…and Katie's eyes widened with dread.

The barn was on fire!

Joshua couldn't resist stealing another glance toward the Lapp farm. He knew he wouldn't see anything in the darkness. Katie was safely in bed. There'd be no lights in either the house or the barn.

Still, he looked in that direction.

He blinked, then blinked again. His eyes must be deceiving him. It couldn't be!

"Katie!"

Without hesitation, he ran.

Flames licked at the edge of the horizon. He offered a quick prayer that Katie wouldn't foolishly rush into a burning barn. The thought that she might gave him a burst of adrenaline and he raced faster than he would have ever believed he could.

He'd reached the lane leading to the Lapp house when he heard it—the loud, ceaseless clanging of the triangle. Katie wasn't inside the barn.

Thank You, God.

When the clanging stopped, he began to worry. She

wouldn't be foolish enough to try to put the flames out by herself, would she?

The horses!

Of course! Katie wouldn't hesitate to try to free the horses.

He pumped his legs harder, ignoring the painful cramping in his thighs. Katie needed him and this time he wasn't going to let her down.

Katie swung the barn door wide and rushed inside as the mama cat and her kittens bolted past her. The frantic whinny of frightened horses made her heart beat double time. Smoke obstructed her view and stole what little breath she had left after her earlier asthma attack. She coughed and bent over at the waist and coughed some more.

She knew the inside of this barn. She could describe every nook and cranny. Unable to see more than a few inches in front of her, she moved by rote to the first stall. She was careful to stand behind the heavy oak gate that Joshua had constructed, knowing that the terrified horse would stampede out of the stall the second it sensed liberty. Sure enough, the horse's thundering hooves pounded the dirt floor as it rushed to freedom. Moving as quickly as she could, she repeated the scenario at the second stall and then the third.

She coughed nonstop now. Her chest burned and she had to fight for every breath. She snatched her inhaler that was pinned to her dress. She couldn't wait until she made it outside. Her lungs felt as if they were going to explode.

She held the inhaler up to her mouth but somebody

grabbed it away and pushed her to the floor. Thick smoke hung in the air above her. Katie turned her face toward the dirt and was able to suck in air instead of smoke. She rolled onto her back to face her assailant.

Levi!

Katie couldn't believe that Levi was her enemy. He must be a victim, too. Hurriedly her eyes scanned the barn. A sinking feeling settled in the pit of her stomach when she realized the truth that was staring her in the face.

"Why?" Katie choked and coughed. "Why, Levi?"

"This land has been in my family for generations. You had no right to it, you sniveling, weak-minded woman. Jacob should have left the farm to me!"

"Levi...please...I need my inhaler." She reached up her hand but clasped only empty air.

"This little thing?" By this time, Levi also choked and coughed on the smoke but he didn't even try to run out the door. "Let's see what happens if I throw this away."

"No! Don't!"

With a laugh that sounded surreal and almost evil, Levi tossed the inhaler into the nearby flames.

"Levi...we have to get out of here."

"You're staying right here where you belong." He laughed again.

Katie crawled on the ground. "We're family." Each word was punctuated with a cough and another gasp for air. Katie clutched the bottom of his pant leg.

Levi viciously kicked her away.

"My brother was family. You were the woman who ruined his life. He'd never have touched a drop of that poison if he'd been happy at home. You killed my brother and you might as well have tried to kill me. You were going to sell the only home I have ever known. I knew when I made my offer that it wasn't enough. I knew you would take one of the greater offers and I couldn't let you do it."

"Why are you burning the barn?"

"To bring down the value of the property. I hoped the other two men would go away."

"Levi, I never told you I would sell to them because I never would. The farm belongs to you."

He glared at her, a flash of uncertainty evident in his expression.

It was so difficult now to breathe that Katie couldn't even feel the crushing pressure of her lungs anymore.

"You knew?" The hoarse whisper that escaped her lips didn't even sound like her voice. "About Jacob's drinking?"

"I knew. And I hated you for it. My brother didn't deserve to die…but you do! May God have mercy on your soul."

"Levi! No! Don't leave me!"

Katie watched Levi disappear into the darkness. She tried to crawl across the floor but was too weak to save herself. Hope was gone. No one would get here in time to help her and she was too weak to save herself. She closed her eyes and surrendered her will to God. If this was His plan, so be it.

A strange heaviness started in her feet and slowly spread up her legs and through her body.

Is this what it feels like to die?

She couldn't draw one more breath.

Her last conscious thought was a deep sadness that she'd never get the chance to see Joshua again. He'd never know she'd forgiven him. She hoped that God would help him forgive himself.

Joshua reached the barn door just as Levi stumbled out of the smoke. He steadied the man and prevented his fall. "Levi, what happened? Are you all right? Where's Katie?"

Joshua glanced over his shoulder hoping he'd see Katie standing on the porch or waiting in the doorway. His heart sank when she wasn't there.

Levi coughed and sputtered and stammered unintelligibly.

"Levi! Get hold of yourself!" He shook the man then shook him again. "Pull yourself together. Where is Katie? Where is she?"

Levi laughed…a maniacal sound that made the hair on the back of Joshua's neck stand up.

"It's too late." Levi laughed again and pointed at the barn, which by now was almost completely engulfed in flames. "She's getting what she deserves."

By now, neighbors had heard the ringing and began to gather in the yard. They started a human chain gathering water from the troughs and passing it one to the other to throw on the fire.

Joshua could hear the distant sound of the fire engines.

But all that registered in his mind were Levi's words. *Katie is in the barn.*

He ripped his shirt off and dipped it into a bucket of water.

"Joshua, what are you doing? You can't go in there."
Amos tried to stop him but Joshua shook his hand away.

"Katie's in there!"

Wrapping his wet shirt around his nose and mouth, he raced into the barn.

Joshua threw an arm up to protect his face. A blast of heat seared his skin.

"Katie!"

He screamed her name but all he could hear was the deafening roar of the fire.

Where was she? He moved farther into the barn. The black, thick smoke obscured his vision and threatened to choke him despite the wet rag on his face.

Where could she be?

Despite the fear that clawed at his gut and the chaos that surrounded him, a voice of reason sounded in Joshua's head. If Katie came into the barn, it would have been to save the horses. Moving quickly, he found his way to the first stall.

"Katie!"

Bending at the waist because of the racking coughs that claimed his body, he made it to the second stall, then the third.

He was about to admit defeat when he tripped over something on the floor and almost fell.

Katie!

Kneeling at her side, he lifted her head. He held two fingers against her throat to feel for a heartbeat and could barely detect one.

Joshua scooped her into his arms. Moving as quickly as he dared, he hurried toward the door. When he burst into the yard, several of the other men came running.

They lifted Katie from his arms and placed her on the ground at the foot of the porch.

A few of the men slapped Joshua on the back and half carried, half dragged him to safety, as well.

The volunteer firefighters, composed of Amish and Englisch alike, fought valiantly to subdue the flames. He knew it wasn't to save the barn—that was futile at this point—but in an attempt to prevent the fire from leaping to the house.

Pushing his way through the crowd, Joshua rushed to Katie and fell to his knees beside her. The paramedics had put an oxygen mask on her face and were preparing to lift her onto a gurney.

"Is she alive?" Joshua wiped soot from his eyes and mouth.

"Barely. We gotta go," said one of the paramedics, who secured an IV bag to a pole on the gurney.

Joshua watched them lift Katie into the ambulance. Sirens rent the night air as the rig sped down the land.

Joshua watched the flashing lights disappear in the distance. He remained on his knees and prayed.

SEVEN

"There you are. C'mon, now. Open those eyes again."

When she did, Katie saw Esther Fischer smoothing the hair off her forehead and away from her face.

"You gave us quite a scare, you know," the bishop's wife said.

"What happened?" Katie's voice was little more than a whispered croak.

"We wanted to ask you the same thing." Joshua appeared in her line of vision. He looked drawn and tired.

"You look horrible." She summoned up a laugh that sounded almost as bad as her gravelly voice.

"*Danki,*" Joshua replied. He moved to the opposite side of the bed and clasped her hand in his. "Maybe that's because I haven't slept in two days."

"*Ya,* that's right," Esther said. "I tried to get him to leave but he's like a mule, stubborn as they come." Esther leaned down and whispered in her ear, "Now we can add loyal and heroic to Joshua Miller's fine qualities. If you don't let him come courting, I might consider asking him myself."

Katie chuckled. "You're already married. What would Amos say?"

"He'd say I was a fine judge of character." Esther patted her arm. "I'm going to go tell the doctor that you are awake."

The door had barely closed behind the woman when Katie turned her eyes toward Joshua.

"I need to tell you—"

"Katie, I—"

Both of them smiled.

"You first," Katie said. Her throat burned and her head throbbed but she'd never been so happy to be alive.

Joshua lifted her hand and pressed her fingers to his lips. Katie's breath caught in her throat when she saw tears form in his eyes.

"I've never prayed so hard in my life." He kissed her fingers again but did not let go of her hand. "I thought it was too late and I'd lost you." He clutched her hand against his chest, tears streaming freely down his face. "Forgive me, Katie, for what I did. I'll spend the rest of my life trying to make it up to you if you'll let me."

Katie lifted her free hand and wiped the tears from his cheek. "I forgive you, Joshua. You know we must forgive as God has forgiven us."

He nodded. "*Ya,* it is the Amish way. But sometimes forgiveness does not come easily."

"How can I blame you for what I was guilty of myself?"

Joshua arched an eyebrow.

"I didn't tell the bishop about Jacob's drinking. Maybe if I had, someone might have been able to help him."

"You cannot blame yourself for his drinking, Katie. It was his responsibility and no one else's fault."

"Really?"

He grinned at the irony of his words. "Like I said, sometimes forgiveness does not come easily. How fortunate we are that God loves us enough to forgive us even when we find it hard to forgive ourselves."

"And Levi?" Her heart felt like a stone in her chest. "What has happened to Levi?"

"He tried to run away. The sheriff arrested him the morning after the fire."

Katie sighed. "I feel sorry for him. To be silent all those years, harbor the belief that I was the cause of his brother's death and yet work sunup till sundown to help me save the farm."

"He was saving the farm for himself, not you, Katie. It was greed that destroyed him."

Katie tried to sit up.

"Here. Let me help you." Joshua slid his arm beneath her shoulders. He lifted her to a sitting position and straightened her pillows to support her back.

Suddenly, he stopped what he was doing. His one arm still rested beneath her shoulders. His other hand gently tilted her chin until her eyes locked with his. Without a word, he lowered his head and captured her lips. When Joshua released her, he removed his arm from her back and straightened up, but he never left her side.

"I wish you had shared your feelings, Joshua, when we were teens. If I'd known how you felt about me…" Her voice trailed off but her eyes never left his face. He didn't squirm and look away like the shy teenage boy he had once been. He stared back at her with a self-confidence she was becoming quite familiar with, an inner strength she found quite appealing.

"You only had eyes for Jacob back then." His eyes darkened with intensity. His smile was slow and lazy.

"And now? If I share my feelings with you now?"

Butterflies danced in her stomach.

"Now?" She gazed into his dark brown eyes and hoped she'd see forever in them.

He leaned his forearms on the hospital rail. "You have to know how I feel about you."

She lowered her eyes. Her heart hammered in her chest as she sensed him moving closer.

"You know I am a man of few words. Always have been. Always will be, I suppose." He tilted her chin up. "So don't listen to my words, Katie. Listen to my heart." He held her hand against his chest.

"I'm listening, Joshua." She placed her hand behind his neck. Her fingers twisted into his thick hair. She pulled him down and moved her lips against his ear. "If I stay still and I listen very hard, what might I hear your heart say?"

Joshua leaned back and grinned.

"It would tell you that I smile every day because I know you're here. It would tell you that it is impossible for me to have one single logical thought because my mind is crowded with thoughts of you."

He kissed her forehead.

"I try to imagine what it would be like to share breakfast with you every morning."

He kissed the tip of her nose.

"I think how *wunderbar* it would be after a long day of work to see you sitting across from me at the dinner table. To talk to you about my day. To listen to you tell me about yours."

His lips touched hers gently, once, twice and then again.

"My heart knows that I think of you in the evenings. In my mind I am holding your hand. I can feel the warmth of your body sitting beside me. I look into your eyes…and I see love…and I feel incredibly blessed."

He gathered her into his arms. "Now do you know how I feel about you?" His husky whisper sent chills up and down her spine. "God has granted me a second chance. I want to spend every day and every night of my life with you. I want us to live on this farm and make it our home. I want to raise a family, a large, noisy, boisterous family, together."

He picked up some strands of her hair and let them run through his fingers, looking at it in awe as though he was watching gold silk. "I hope our *kinner* will have hair as silky and bright as yours."

His expression sobered and he stared at her, his eyes revealing a hint of vulnerability.

"I want to grow old with you, Katie. And I intend to thank God every day of my life for that blessing if you'll have me."

Tears of happiness shimmered in her eyes. Real love had nothing to do with trying to control the life of another. Love was about trust and sharing and compromise. It was putting your partner's wants and needs first but not at the cost of sacrificing your own.

She looked into Joshua's face and she knew. She loved this man and she always would.

"How many *kinner* did you say we are going to have?"

A wide grin broke out on Joshua's face. "Four? Five?"

She tightened her hold on his neck and drew him closer. "Then we better not waste any more time." She kissed him with all the promise of a future she held in her heart.

"You will marry me?" Joshua asked.

Katie's heart felt as if it might burst. "Yes, Joshua. I will marry you."

Joshua let out an excited whoop. "When, Katie?"

"This is November, Joshua, is it not?"

He nodded.

"November is the month we hold our Amish weddings. The harvest is over and spring planting has not yet begun. It is the perfect time, Joshua. Don't you think?"

The look in his eyes took her breath away.

"I couldn't think of a better time, *lieb*. I love you, Katie."

"And I love you."

Beneath his kiss, Katie could feel her lips bow into a demure, satisfied smile.

It was true. Joshua Miller was a man of few words— but when he spoke from his heart, his words were indeed powerful and of great importance.

Danki, God.

* * * * *

Dear Reader,

Amish books are so popular with readers that Amish fiction is becoming its own genre. In this high-tech world of computers, tablets and smartphones it seems to fascinate people that there are still communities in this country that do not have electricity or television or radios and yet live fulfilling, quality lives.

I myself have always admired the Amish. They represent to me a simpler time, a slice of days past when God and family were the two most important relationships in a person's life and families stayed together in the same community. Sometimes in this day and age where relatives are split or scattered and employment stresses, money worries and health issues can make us forget these quieter, uncomplicated eras, it feels good to escape in a book and travel back to a more peaceful time and place.

However, the Amish are human just like the rest of us. They struggle with the same temptations and negative feelings that we all face. So this novella explored some of those human issues touching on jealousy, greed, alcoholism and abuse.

I think seeing that the Amish struggle with the same issues many of us deal with helps us respect the way they handle their lives. Their strong belief in God and their devotion to family show by example that a person with human flaws can still garner strength from God, find forgiveness and devote their lives to following His word.

I hope you enjoyed this story. I would love to hear from my readers and I can be reached at diane@dianeburkeauthor.com.

Blessings,
Diane Burke

Questions for Discussion

1. The general public rarely hears of Amish committing serious crimes. Yet, the Amish people wrestle with the same temptations as all the rest of us. How do you think they handle their temptations? How can we benefit from the Amish example and yet still live in a worldly world?

2. What scene, if any, in the story moved you and why? Who was your favorite character and what was it you liked about him or her?

3. Many people can forgive others much faster than they can forgive themselves. Why do you think that is?

4. Do you think Joshua should have told the bishop about Jacob's drinking? Why or why not?

5. Many spouses accept abuse, either emotional or physical, from their partner and remain silent about it. Have you ever known anyone in these circumstances? How did they cope with it and do you think it was dealt with correctly or not?

RETURN TO
WILLOW TRACE

Kit Wilkinson

To my son, Jonah, who is wise beyond his years.
May the Lord bless you with abundant love.
You and Charlie are my greatest joy.

Let love and faithfulness never leave you.
—*Proverbs* 3:3

ONE

"Good night, Bishop Miller. See you next week." Lydia Stoltz waved a quick goodbye with her cleaning rag. The old Amish man shuffled out the front doors of his furniture store, placing his black felt hat atop a nest of soft, silvery hair. A strong autumn wind blew against the glass doors. Lydia wrestled to get them closed, but not before a few orange and yellow leaves rolled under the skirt of her dark purple frock. An autumn storm was brewing on the western horizon. Cold north winds clashed with some lingering rain clouds. A quick, violent tempest was on the way.

She bolted the big steel lock and drew the long green shade over the length of the doors. Miller's Original Amish Furniture—Closed, it read on the other side. Bishop Miller owned and operated both a lumber mill, which his son Eli had recently taken over, and the furniture store. Together, they formed the largest Amish-owned businesses not only in Willow Trace, but in all of Lancaster County. People from all over trusted the name Miller and purchased their plain but sturdy wooden furniture from this store.

Lydia collected the leaves from the floor and resumed her work. It was the same each Wednesday.
After hours, she would clean Miller's storefront, making the wood of each display piece gleam with the same
care with which they'd been handcrafted in the workshop attached to the store. Afterward, she walked the
short distance home, where she and her mother raised
rabbits, sheep and miniature horses on a small farm that
had been in her father's family for generations. It was
hard work for just the two of them, and sometimes sales
were low, hence the job at the furniture store. But Lydia
loved the farm, and ever since her father had abandoned
them, she had taken it upon herself to make sure that
the beautiful place didn't slip through their fingers.

Lydia hadn't taken two steps from the doors when the
dead bolt of the front door snapped open. She started,
nearly dropping her cleaning rag. Again, cold air swept
around her, and the strings of her white prayer *kapp*
danced on her shoulders.

"I forgot to mention somethin' to ye." Old Bishop
Miller craned his head through the tiny space between
the double doors.

Lydia expelled the quick breath of air she'd held in
and laughed at her own silly nervousness. "Oh dear.
You gave me quite a fright."

"I'm sorry for that, but you should know that one of
the craftsmen is still in the shop, working late. I didn't
want him to frighten ye. You might hear him banging
around back there."

Lydia nodded. It happened from time to time that

one of the craftsmen worked late to finish a piece that had been preordered. With Christmas only two months away, she imagined there was quite a demand.

"Mr. Yoder. Joseph Yoder. I believe you know each other." A sly grin fell over the bishop's face. "Good night, Miss Lydia." He pulled the doors closed again and turned the lock over himself.

Joseph Yoder? Oh yeah. I know him, all right. She had courted him. Thankfully, for the past five years, she'd seldom heard his name. No one in her Ordnung had spoken much of him after he'd sped off to Indiana five years ago.

Lydia's heart beat heavily against her rib cage. She slung her dirty rag into the cleaning bucket, trudged to the closet and snatched up the broom. With sweeping, it was best to begin in the back corner and work across, moving with the grain of the wood floors. Her movements were sharp, fueled by her own emotions. Buried sentiments churned up like the dust that blew across the floor.

Just last week, Lydia had heard some gossip that Joseph would be back for his cousin's wedding. Perhaps if she had bothered to ask more questions she would have found out that he was crafting furniture at Miller's shop while he was home. But she hadn't. Lydia had vowed long ago that she would not allow herself to be interested in anything that had to do with Joseph Yoder.

For Lydia there were two kinds of men—the kind who kept promises and the kind who did not. Running off without so much as a word after promising to love her forever put Joseph into the latter category. Lydia knew all too well, from experience with her own unreliable father, that she would rather be alone than live a life with a man who could disappear without a word of explanation.

No, Lydia had quit thinking about Joseph's soft hazel eyes and broad shoulders. She'd forgotten his hearty laugh and mischievous smile. She'd even courted Gideon Lapp for a short spell. And while the five years that had passed had dulled the burn of Joseph's abandonment, there were embers enough left to singe her when she thought on it for too long.

And now here he was so close. Although with the huge steel warehouse walls between them, they would stay quite separate. So why were her knees trembling and her heart palpitating as if she'd run a marathon?

Lydia swept the pile of dirt into a dustpan and dumped it into the garbage. Now, on to polishing—that was a job she quite enjoyed. She passed her oiled cloth over each surface, between every groove until all the wood shone bright and clean. She admired the work of the Amish craftsmen and agreed that those who worked for Bishop Miller were among the most skilled.

Of course, it was wrong to be prideful, but Lydia saw no fault in appreciating the useful pieces. Surely there were no others in the world that compared. She could not imagine any more functional or sturdy than the ones in this showroom.

Wind whistled around the metal warehouse and across the storefront. The storm outside had grown strong. Eerie sounds echoed through the building. The front and side windows pinged as a sudden downpour let loose. Lydia hastened her work, setting her pace to the heavy droplets as they hammered in rhythm against the building.

The sooner she got home the better. For many reasons. Already that day, she and her mother had worked hard in the stables, and her limbs trembled with fatigue. Now there was the storm, which would drench her on the way home. And last but not least, Joseph Yoder stood only a few feet away. Did he know she was there? What if he did? What if he came to talk to her?

Boom. A loud noise caused Lydia to jump. What was the matter with her? She closed her eyes and took a deep breath. It was nothing. The storm. The wind. A box or some sort of loose rubbish blown up against the front doors. She needn't be so edgy.

Lydia resumed her cleaning. But again, something crashed against the front doors and they shook. *That is some strong wind.* Perhaps Bishop Miller had not pulled the doors completely shut. She went forward to check, reaching for the key, which she kept in a small pouch attached to her wrist.

As she moved, the doors continued to rattle—loud and steady. *That* could not be the wind. She supposed she'd known that all along, but what *was* on the other side of the doors? She could not imagine.

Her hands trembled as she tugged at the big green shade. It rolled up with a snap. Lydia screamed and scrambled back. On the other side of the door, a large man pressed hard against the glass. He looked disheveled. His eyes were translucent. His long, thin face was framed with dark matted hair and stained with blood. In his hand, he grasped a black pistol, which he held pointed at her head.

He scratched the glass with the barrel of the weapon. Lydia let out another bloodcurling scream. Clambering back again, she collided with a solid piece of furniture and fought to keep her balance.

"Open up. Come on. Now!" The look on his face was savage.

Lydia didn't move. She couldn't. Fear paralyzed her. This was a way bigger problem than facing Joseph Yoder.

Oh dear Lord, what can I do?

Joseph Yoder laid aside the small chisel. He took up some fine sandpaper, and with long, steady strokes, he smoothed the slots he'd carved out of the surface of the large armoire he'd promise to finish for Bishop Miller.

With a grunt, he lifted the heavy door and lined up the corresponding slots to their hinges. His tired muscles quaked under the weight and he was forced to lower it back to the ground. He could not finish the armoire alone. Even if he'd managed to get the door in place, he didn't have the strength and balance to hold it up with one hand while placing the pins with the other.

He thought of Lydia on the other side of the building. Bishop Miller had mentioned she would be cleaning the storefront that evening. She could help put the pins in. Not that he would dare ask her. She wouldn't want to see him, and he didn't care to see her, either.

Joseph ran his callused fingers over the fine armoire. *Ya,* even Lydia would approve of this work.

That is, until she found out it was his.

Joseph sighed and wiped the sweat from his brow with a clean cloth. Time for a short break. His hands shook from the long hours put in over the past three days. He needed some nourishment. Maybe food would calm the butterflies twittering in his stomach…even though he was pretty certain they were not caused by hunger.

He sat down with the fresh rolls and thick slices of smoked ham that his nana had packed for him. It was good to be home, even though it was only for a few weeks. After that, he would be anxious to get back to his uncle Toby's in Indiana. Joseph had wondered if he'd see Lydia while he was home and if he did whether she would speak to him or not. She had cut off all communication with him after he'd left Willow Trace. He had been devastated. But his family convinced him it was God's will for him to be in Indiana. Over time, he came to agree with them. Especially once he heard Lydia had so quickly moved on to court Gideon Lapp. As far as he knew, she was getting married herself this wedding season. So what did he care? One day, he would do the same once he'd settled in with his uncle's business.

The wind and rain slammed hard against the metal building. This severe of a storm had not been expected. He thought of Lydia having to walk home in all that rain. She didn't live far, but anyone would get soaked to the bone on a night like tonight. He must offer his buggy. It was the proper thing to do. The butterflies in his stomach felt more like hummingbirds as he crossed the large workshop. He knocked gently at the back door leading into the storefront. Bishop Miller had locked it, or perhaps it was locked all of the time. Maybe Lydia would have a key?

In any case, there was no answer.

He wrapped his knuckles again against the wooden door, a little louder this time.

Still, there was no answer. But Lydia had to be there. The shop's oil-powered lights were on. Their bright rays shone across the threshold and spread over the tops of his leather shoes.

"Lydia?" He shook the handle. "I don't mean to bother you. Just thought you could take my buggy home. Can you hear me? Lydia?"

He waited. At long last, he heard something, but it was not what he expected. There was movement. Scuffling. A loud shriek. Joseph swallowed hard. That scream…that was Lydia. He knew her voice, even when it was hysterical—and that was a rare thing for a woman like Lydia. He couldn't imagine what she could be screaming about. A mouse? A spider, maybe?

No. Lydia would never be frightened by a little critter. She was not the type of woman to scream over something like that. Joseph's throat sunk to his stomach.

"Lydia? Can you open the door? Please? Are you okay? Lydia?" He shook the door.

Nothing. All was silent and the door would not budge.

Panic struck through him. He would have to get into the store another way. Lydia was in trouble. And he was going to help her whether she welcomed him or not.

TWO

Joseph raced into Bishop Miller's office. Surely the old man kept an extra key inside. But at seeing the multiple stacks of papers piled over cabinets and tables, Joseph decided it might take forever to find a key in that mess. The fastest way to get to Lydia was to go out the back door and run around to the front of the store.

Joseph wove his way through the maze of unfinished furniture and pushed through the heavy metal doors in back. Through pelting rain, he sprinted around the corner, his chest tight and heart pounding. His foot slipped on the loose gravel. Sharp rocks pressed into his palms as he pushed off the ground and kept moving. He turned the corner from the side of the building. A distant streetlight glowed over the facade of the store. He saw no cars in the parking lot. No traffic on the main road. Only darkness lay beyond the scope of the lights.

Joseph slowed his steps, approaching the big glass doors. Lydia's voice sounded faintly under the din of pouring rain. He froze as she came into view. She was crying. Sobbing. In front of her lurched a tall, dark-headed man. He was soaked from the rain and his coat was stained with…

Was that blood?

It looked like blood. The man jerked toward Lydia. Light reflected off something he held in his hand. Joseph flinched. It was a gun.

Please, Lord, don't let me have been too late, Joseph prayed as he pressed his way through the front doors. Lydia lifted her head. Her eyes were wide with fear.

"Put the gun away and step back, sir." Joseph spoke in a controlled voice as he entered the store and continued forward.

The man turned with great effort, groaning as he moved. Even his breath was labored. The gun fell to the floor. Then with his limp arms dangling at his sides, he closed his eyes and collapsed to the floor.

Joseph rushed forward and knelt over the fallen man. "What's happened? How did he get in here?"

"Joseph, it's okay." Lydia knelt beside him. "It's Billy Ferris. I let him in. He's hurt and confused."

Billy. The same Billy who'd been the reason Joseph had left the little town of Willow Trace. And left Lydia. Joseph clenched his teeth. He looked down at the man's face. Bruised, swollen, cut, bleeding, his features bore no resemblance to the Englisch boy he'd spent so much of his childhood with. *Could this really be Billy?*

Joseph reached forward and touched the man's shoulder. His eyes flickered. The man jerked forward again, grabbing at his belly.

"Joe…" He coughed. He looked up and attempted to smile at Joseph. Only then did Joseph believe that this wreck of a person was indeed his old friend.

Lydia leaned in and touched Joseph's shoulder. Her whole body trembled. "He's bleeding badly. I think he has a fever, too. He keeps trying to say something but I can't understand."

Joseph turned to Lydia. Looking into her eyes for the first time in five years caused a flood of unexpected emotions to race through him. Love, tenderness, pain and betrayal. But that would all have to wait. Billy Ferris was between them, once again.

"How is he hurt?" Joseph examined his old friend limp on the floor. At his shoulder, there was a cut, more like a slash. His clothing was soaked from the ribs down with not only rain but with blood and dirt, as well. From the way he clutched at his belly, the pain there must have been most acute. Joseph lifted the tails of the bloody shirt and cringed at what had once been a tightly muscled abdomen. Billy's stomach had been cut. Lydia gasped and turned her head away.

It was no small wound. No wonder Billy was grabbing at his belly. He needed a doctor. "Is there a phone? We have to call 911."

Lydia shook her head. "I don't have one. The store doesn't have one. Bishop Miller won't allow them. He pays for an outside service to take orders for the store. Messages are hand delivered."

"I don't have one, either." Joseph sat back on his heels. What could they do? The closest place was Lydia's but he couldn't imagine moving Billy in his buggy in this condition.

"Can you get some water and rags?" he asked Lydia. "Maybe if we clean him up a bit, we will see that he's not quite so bad."

"*Ya,* okay." She hopped up and headed to the back of the store.

Joseph gazed down. "What happened to you, my friend?"

Billy murmured and coughed. His eyes looked up. The pain Joseph could see in them nearly brought him to tears. Billy clutched Joseph's wrist and tried again to speak.

"You have a phone, don't you?" *Of course he does.* Joseph searched Billy's pockets. He found a set of keys, a wallet and a plastic Baggie of pink powder. The label over the packet read Bath Salts. Joseph frowned. Bath salts must be some type of street drug. He tossed the bag aside. Looked as if Billy's bad choices had only gotten worse since Joseph went to Indiana. Now here he was cut and possibly bleeding to death.

"What happened to you, Billy?" Joseph grabbed a sheet draped over a nearby piece of furniture. He rolled it up and placed it under Billy's head in an attempt to make him more comfortable. "You should have gone to the hospital, not come here.... Why are you here?"

Billy tried again to speak. "Lydia... What's..."

Joseph frowned. *Lydia? Lydia and Billy? Friends?* A twinge of resentment flashed over him. Was that why Billy was there? To see Lydia?

Lydia returned with towels and water. She placed one towel on Billy's stomach then pressed another to the deep cut on his shoulder. Joseph helped inch Billy's arm out of the jacket so that she could get to the cut better. The patient protested with a groan.

"He said that he came here to see you?" Joseph wished he'd checked his emotions before speaking. Had he sounded jealous?

Lydia shrugged. "I guess. That's what it sounded

like he said to me, but I don't know why. I haven't laid eyes on him since—well—since that last night we all went out together."

That last night. Joseph knew all too well the night she meant. It had been the worst of his life. The night his parents sent him away to Indiana without letting him speak to Lydia.

Remembering it was like getting his own stomach cut open, although it was more like his heart that had been shred to pieces.

"Talk to us, Billy," Joseph said. "Who did this to you? How did this happen? Why? Why didn't you go to the hospital?"

Billy's lips trembled in a feverish delirium. "He knows—he knows—and he'll find you. What's… Remember Alex? Be…be careful."

He knows? Who knows? Who is Alex? Lydia was right. Billy's words made no sense. Whether his mind was affected by drugs or by the horrible pain, only a doctor could discern.

The cut on Billy's shoulder was much worse than it had appeared. Joseph rolled up the sleeve of his heavy coat to help elevate the wound. Something hard and metal was inside the sleeve. It had perhaps stopped the blade from causing further damage. Joseph groped inside the coat sleeve. He hadn't thought to check there for a pocket. Amish didn't have fancy things like pockets. He hoped it wasn't full of drugs. It wasn't. Joseph nearly smiled as he slid a high-tech touch-screen cell phone from the coat sleeve. He tapped the emergency button and held it until a dial tone sounded.

A voice answered quickly. "This is Emergency. Please state your name and location…"

Joseph and Lydia exchanged a look of hope.

Thank You, Lord. Thank You. Please let Billy live.

The next forty minutes seemed an eternity to Lydia. Bright lights flashed, sirens whistled, the rain continued to pour down. People ran here and scurried there. It was as if she were in a dream where the images were all blurred and fuzzy—a dream she wished she'd wake from, making this strange evening all go away.

Instead, she watched as the EMTs strapped Billy Ferris to a gurney. They gave him several injections and hooked him to an oxygen tank. Lydia closed her eyes, hoping to hold in the tears, which had perched on her bottom lids. Her own chest was tight and lacked sufficient air. Only adrenaline had kept her from feeling the full weight of the situation. But now that Billy was someone else's responsibility, exhaustion and confusion slammed down on her like a hammer.

And that was without even thinking about the fact that, after all these years, Joseph Yoder was back in Willow Trace and standing right beside her. So many emotions flooded through her—too many to sort. What was clear, however, was that, during his absence, Joseph had grown taller, broader and more handsome. His hands were now lined with calluses. His face had a crease or two developing around the eyes. His brown hair was still wavy and streaked with honey-blond strands. His soft hazel eyes looked as if they might take her in and swallow her up whole.

For a second, there'd been a glimpse of that same boy

who'd loved her since grade school, but then Joseph's expression had become guarded. She wondered if he saw changes in her. Not that it mattered. What she and Joseph had had was gone. Forever.

"Miss Stoltz, I have just a few more questions."

Lydia turned to Detective Macy, the man addressing her. Several officers had arrived at the store, but this one seemed to be in charge. He wanted to know every detail of what had happened. The Amish, in general, didn't care much for the Englisch law enforcement— but they had to be there. Billy was, of course, Englisch. She tried to oblige Macy's unending questions, but since she and Joseph had had nothing to do with Billy, his wounds or his arrival to the store, she didn't see how anything she said was the least bit helpful.

"Did Mr. Ferris give you a reason for coming to the furniture store?" Macy asked. "Did he know that you would be here?"

"He tried to say a few things, but I cannot tell you that I understood any of it. I have no idea if he knew I worked here or not. I haven't seen him in years." Lydia thought, too, about Bishop Miller. He would not be pleased about all this transpiring at his store. He might even question her judgment in friends. Thanks to her father, she and her mother had enough to prove to the community without adding something else to it. In any case, this was going to be all over the papers and the evening news, as was anything both newsworthy and Amish.

Joseph ran his oil-stained hands over his thick hair and sighed aloud. He longed to be away from this chaos.

How had this happened? He'd imagined seeing Lydia again for the first time in many different scenarios— at his cousin's wedding, at her farmhouse, at Sunday meeting. But he had never imagined it like this.

"I didn't really understand him, either." Joseph fiddled with the straw hat between his hands. "But he was certainly trying to talk. He recognized me. He said my name. But he couldn't have known that I would be here tonight. I decided to work late just a few hours ago."

Macy tapped some notes into his electronic notepad with a tiny stylus. Then he turned back to Lydia. "So, you and Mr. Ferris were friends? He came here to see you?"

Lydia's eyes widened and her cheeks reddened. "No. We were never friends. Those two were friends." She pointed at him. "I haven't spoken to Billy Ferris since I last saw Joseph. And that was summer five years ago."

Joseph wondered if Macy could detect the bitterness in her voice. To him, it seemed unmistakable. "It's true. He was a *gut* friend…before I moved away. He is Englisch, but my family lived next door to his. We—we grew up together…so to speak. But truthfully, I haven't heard a word from him in the past five years. And like Lydia, I haven't seen him since that same night that she mentioned—the one before I moved to Indiana."

Macy scrunched his face, as if he'd tasted something sour. "So, you are both saying that you haven't seen each other or Mr. Ferris since you were all together on the very same night five years ago?"

It did sound kind of strange when he put it like that, Joseph thought.

"*Ya,* I suppose that is true." Joseph scratched his head.

"Did anything special happen on that night?" Macy looked suspicious.

Lydia tensed. For an instant, Joseph thought to reach over and touch his hand to hers and comfort her. But those days were over. Perhaps seeing her brought old habits back to mind.

"It was back in our *rumspringa* days," Joseph said. "A long time ago. We met some Englisch kids and had some beer."

"Where did you meet?"

A bead of sweat formed on Joseph's forehead. He wiped it with his sleeve and swallowed hard. He knew Lydia didn't want to hear any of this. He didn't care to talk about it, either. "Tucker's Pond. It was mostly friends of Billy's. We were the only Amish. The two of us left pretty early on."

"And that's it?" Macy tapped more notes into his electronic tablet.

Lydia nudged her head at Joseph as if saying to go on with the rest of the story.

Joseph shifted his weight, hesitating before continuing. "So, there is a bit more. Just before we left, Billy took out some drugs. I have no idea what they were. We didn't take them, but most of the others did. After a half hour or so, one of the girls became very ill. When that happened, Billy got all agitated. He wouldn't let us help. He told us to leave so I took Lydia home."

"Agitated?"

"Angry. Excited. Worried about the girl, I think. But he was high, too. It's hard to say."

Detective Macy stared up at the ceiling for a second, as if stowing away this bit of information in case he needed it later. Then he looked at Lydia. "And this is how you remember it, too?"

Lydia nodded, her head down.

"Who was this girl? Do you remember any of their names?"

Lydia and Joseph exchanged a quick glance.

"They were Billy's friends. We didn't know them," Joseph said.

"I remember one," Lydia said. "One of the girl was named Michelle. Not the one who was sick. Another. She had been out with us before. But not the others. Do you think this has something to do with what happened tonight?"

Macy shook his head. "I doubt it. My guess is that this is all about drug sales. A deal gone bad. Your friend Mr. Ferris has been arrested several times on suspicion of selling and distribution. I have a feeling this will be connected with a more recent incident. But stay away from Tucker's Pond. It's still a high school hangout and a place to buy and sell."

"Yes, sir."

"Well…thank you." Macy looked over his notes and seemed pleased. "That will be all for now. I'll just need to know how to get in touch with you, if I have more questions."

They each rattled off their addresses. As he typed them into the pad, his phone began to ring.

"Excuse me." He took the call and began to circle the shop, moving away from them. Joseph and Lydia stood like statues at the front door until he returned.

"Bad news." Macy put his phone away. "I'm sorry to have to tell you this…. Mr. Ferris passed away on the ride to the hospital. I'll notify the next of kin. You should go on home and be very careful. Remember, unless the medical examiner thinks the cuts were self-inflicted, this is now a homicide. Neither of you should leave town without permission. Marked cars will be patrolling here on a regular basis until we know more. This is for your own safety and protection. I can arrange an escort home, if you like."

"That won't be necessary," Lydia said quickly. The detective turned away and dismissed them with a nod.

"Wait…Detective Macy, do you believe we are in danger?" Joseph asked.

Detective Macy looked back. "Do you think you are in danger, Mr. Yoder?"

"I don't know that I know what to think," Joseph said.

Despite her brave stance, Lydia was fighting an onslaught of tears. "It doesn't make any sense. None of it. But we do think Billy told us to be careful, or at least, it seemed like he was trying to say that."

"Then you should be careful, even if it makes no sense. One of the hardest parts of my job," Detective Macy said, "is to remind myself that with every senseless murder there is a killer somewhere who thinks it all makes perfect sense."

THREE

Joseph and Lydia hardly spoke to one another as they locked up the store. Out back, she waited inside the buggy while Joseph hitched up his chestnut mare. *Ten minutes.* She could handle Joseph Yoder for ten more minutes. That was all it would take for him to get her home. Ten more minutes. Lydia stiffened as Joseph came around to the front of the buggy and gave her a nod.

"Thankfully, the rain has died down a bit, *ya?*" He climbed inside the vehicle. It was a four-seater, hard covered buggy—the type Amish families used to go to Sunday meeting. He tapped the reins and called gently to his horse. The mare stepped out onto the main road toward home.

The steady trotting and Joseph at her side made Lydia think of many courting nights that had started or ended in this way.

"A most unusual night," she said. "I can hardly believe any of it actually happened."

"Poor Billy. He should have stopped that business of his long ago."

"What business?"

"Selling drugs. I found some on him when I was searching for a phone. But I didn't know it had gone so far. I didn't know he had a record. What a shame. He was a good guy—I mean, inside him somewhere, he had a good heart." Joseph wiped the couple of tears that trickled down his cheek.

"*Ya,* it is sad." Lydia touched his shoulder. The contact made her suddenly aware of her natural attraction to him. She wondered how her body could betray her heart like that. "I saw you give the bag to the police.... So, you really hadn't talked to Billy since you left?" The question sounded like an accusation. She hadn't meant for it to, but he and Billy had been so close. It seemed so strange they hadn't been in touch.

"Didn't you read any of my letters?"

Lydia dropped her hand and lowered her head. No. She had not read them. It was too painful. And what was the point? He'd left without a word. Just like her father. His decision about her had been clear enough. No need to read his letters and feel the pain all over again. "I did not. You left. End of story."

Joseph let out a sigh. "It wasn't like that. It wasn't like that at all."

So, what was it like? There was a sadness in his voice, but she ignored it. "Why are we even talking about that? After all that has happened tonight? We should be praying for Billy's family. We should be asking ourselves why God chose us to be with Billy in his last moments. I feel some sort of responsibility in this, don't you?"

"You are right, Lydia." Joseph tilted his head, as if reflecting on her questions. "But it's all so strange. If neither of us has seen nor heard from him in all this time, it makes me wonder if he wasn't wounded near the store and stumbled into the first place he passed. Doesn't that make more sense than him actually looking for you or for me? Maybe what Billy was mumbling had no meaning or purpose at all?"

Lydia's mind flashed over the moment she'd pulled up the shade and seen this half-dead person clinging so desperately to the front doors. "I know. It's so strange that he was there. How did he get there? There was no car."

"No. I didn't see a car, either."

She nodded. "Do you think Macy will ask us more questions?"

Joseph shrugged. "I don't see why. We told him everything we know. I think he will concentrate on Billy's drug connections."

A cold chill passed down Lydia's spine. She pulled her wool shawl tighter around her shoulders. "This is such a tragedy. It will bring grief to the whole community."

After ten long minutes, they passed over the small bridge and up Holly Hill to the farmhouse where she and her mother lived. He slowed the buggy as they approached the old gray-stone-and-white-clapboard house. He halted the mare and hopped out. She jumped out, too. She did not want Joseph Yoder walking her up to the porch. It was too much like a visit to the past, too much like reliving their outings in Joseph's old courting buggy.

But she wasn't quick enough. There he was, standing at the passenger side with an umbrella in hand. He held it over her head as they walked together up the front stairs. His shoulder brushed against hers and she tensed.

When they reached the top stair, the front porch illuminated, flooding them in soft yellow light. Like most Amish farms in Willow Trace, Holly Hill used an oil-powered generator to run a refrigerator, some other small appliances and a few overhead lights. Her mother's silhouette appeared at the screen door. Naomi had been waiting up, probably surprised to hear the sounds of a buggy in her gravel drive.

"Hello, Mrs. Stoltz. *Gut* to see you. I'm seeing Lydia home in the rain. We had a bit of an—"

"Joseph Yoder!" Naomi flew onto the porch. "Now, if you aren't a sight for sore eyes. Come give this old woman a hug."

Lydia sighed. She was afraid the enthusiasm might encourage Joseph to stay longer. She certainly didn't want that.

"Please come in. Have some cake and hot tea before heading home," her mother said.

Lydia grunted silently in protest. She did not want to spend any more time than necessary in the presence of Joseph Yoder.

He, on the other hand, seemed pleased enough. "That would be just fine. I haven't had much to eat since lunch."

Mrs. Stoltz cut generous slices of pumpkin bread and poured steaming-hot cinnamon-spiced tea for each of them. They gathered around the small kitchen table, holding hands, and prayed for their food.

Joseph slid out a chair at the head of the table.

"Not there," her *mamm* said. "That's Jonathan's place."

"Oh, yes. I'm sorry." Joseph's eyes searched Lydia's as he moved quickly to another spot at the table.

Heat rushed to Lydia's cheeks. While she admired her mother's capability to forgive and to hope, she felt only anger toward her father. Where the gesture was an expression of Naomi's love and her faith in God to sustain her, for Lydia, the empty place at the table was a reminder of her pain.

As was seeing Joseph again. Which was exactly why she would maintain her distance during his visit. She had hoped to avoid him altogether, but with him working for Bishop Miller and with the evening's tragedy, who knew how much they might be forced to be together?

Lydia swallowed away the lump of emotion in her throat. She turned to her mother and provided details of their encounter with Billy Ferris and what occurred afterward.

"I can't believe it." Her *mamm* shook her head. "Such a young man. And so well liked by everyone."

"*Ya.* Who would want to kill him?" Lydia said.

"The detective seemed to think it related to his selling drugs." Joseph rinsed his cake down with a cup of tea.

"Oh dear." Her mother let out a deep sigh. "Well, it is all business for the Englisch to deal with. You must put it behind you. Let the past be passed."

Her mother patted Joseph's hand and looked at both of them in turn. There was nothing subtle in her message, which was not about Billy's death. "At least it's nice to see the two of you together again. After all these years."

Joseph stood abruptly. "I should be getting home now. It's late. Thank you, Mrs. Stoltz. Lydia."

He took his hat from the wooden pin on the wall where he'd hung it earlier. He placed it on his head. "I'll let you know when the funeral arrangements have been made."

Lydia stared at the floor as Joseph left through the kitchen door. Then, in the shadows of the dining room window, she watched him climb into the buggy and set off down the lane. It was a little ritual from their courting days. Filled with warm and tender love, she'd watch him disappear over Holly Hill.

Tonight there was no tender warmth. She felt only the memory of heartache cutting through her.

There were a couple of reasons why Lydia returned to the furniture store on Friday afternoon. For one, she had not been back to complete her cleaning. Now that the police had finish their work, the storefront really needed a scrubbing. But also Lydia had thought that by coming earlier in the day she could avoid running into Joseph. He would be busy in the back and not even know she was there. In any case, she'd see him soon enough when he drove her to Billy's funeral the following day.

"I didn't expect you, Miss Lydia." Bishop Miller stepped up to the front of the shop when the little bell rang over the front door.

"I'm just finishing up my cleaning from Wednesday. Mamm and I got our chores done early today, so

I hope you don't mind. I know it must need a thorough going-over."

"Of course not. Should I let Mr. Yoder know that you're here?" The old man gave her his sly grin again.

Lydia forced a frown and shook her head. "I don't think that will be necessary. I won't be staying long."

It was hard wiping away the remaining traces of blood where poor Billy had spent some of his last moments. In a way, the act of cleansing wasn't merely physical; it helped to process the terrifying events of that evening. Then tomorrow she would face her sorrow at the funeral. *The Lord gives, and the Lord takes away. Blessed be the name of the Lord.* Life's events didn't always make sense, but as she'd been taught, she accepted them as the will of the Lord.

Lydia was running her cloth over the last few pieces of furniture and humming when the bell over the shop door rang. She stopped and looked up.

"Mr. Bowman." Bishop Miller offered his hand. "What business brings you here today?"

"Please, Levi, we've known each other for years. Call me Hank." They shook hands. Lydia turned away and went back to her work.

"Well, first I came to say that Mr. Ferris was my restaurant manager and a good friend," the large man said.

Lydia couldn't help but overhear.

"I'm very sorry for your loss," Bishop Miller said. "Such a sad, sad business."

"Billy was a good man. I don't know what happened to him getting involved in drugs. If there were any damages to your store, I am happy to cover the cost."

"That won't be necessary. But I thank ye for the offer."

"I also heard that some of your employees were here and had to deal with him. Please pass on my gratitude for calling 911 and trying to help him. It must have been terrifying for them to see a man in such a state."

Lydia ducked behind a large piece of furniture. She didn't want to talk again about what had happened that night and she feared the Bishop might call her over for an introduction.

"Well, they knew Mr. Ferris." The Bishop's voice filled the room. "Lydia and Joseph. Would you like to speak to them?"

"Oh, no, no. That's not necessary. If they were his friends, then I'll see them tomorrow at the funeral. I do have one other order of business, however. Billy used an Amish furniture maker to build all the tables we have in the restaurant front. I'd like to order twenty more for our back room."

"I'm afraid Mr. Ferris didn't order them from here," Bishop Miller said.

"Well, I like to buy local when I can, and of course, you're local and original."

Miller nodded. "Then I'll send one of my craftsmen over and you can show him what you would like. First thing Monday morning."

Bowman shook the Bishop's hand again and left the store. Then he called Joseph to the storefront. Lydia put away her cleaning. Her first encounter with Joseph had been so difficult. She need not put herself through more than necessary.

But he was too quick. She sensed him enter the showroom. She looked up as he approach the bishop.

His face glistened with hard work and the front of his trousers was sprinkled with sawdust. He had never looked more handsome. He smiled at her and her pulse raced. Lydia nodded to them both then escaped through the front doors. She scurried across the parking lot, crossed the highway and fled into the woods. She would take the long way home following an old path that led to her stable. The fresh air and exercise would set her right.

Joseph listened halfheartedly to Bishop Miller as he asked again about his uncle's furniture business in Indiana, about the mess with Billy Ferris the other night and then about making tables for some restaurant in town. But most of his thoughts were on Lydia. She had just grabbed her shawl and headed out of the store. His eyes followed her petite figure to the edge of the woods across the street. With a smile, he remembered many times walking alongside her, relaxing in the low afternoon sun. Now it was only tension that seemed to live between them.

"I have done some tables like this before," Joseph answered the bishop. "But I won't have time to make twenty of them before I go back to Indiana. Better put one of your other craftsmen on it."

"*Ach.* They won't want to do it, either." Bishop Miller slapped Joseph on the shoulder and let out a loud chuckle. "I'll tell Mr. Bowman that it will have to wait until after the Christmas rush. But we will not worry about that now. But you, young man, it's Friday afternoon. Put down your tools and go home. You're buried in work. You're too young fer that. You should be thinking about marriage and family—not just furniture, my boy."

He wasn't positive, but the old man seemed to be looking out the window toward Lydia's place as he spoke. Or was that his imagination? Joseph nodded and turned back toward his workstation.

Lydia stopped and turned in a circle on the forest path. The wind blew hard, and small animals scurried over the leaf-covered ground. She had walked through these woods a million times, played in them, even hidden there from her parents on occasion when she was younger. She loved the forest. She felt close to God, breathing in the fresh air, listening to the quick waters of the brook and watching the intermittent rays of sunlight dancing through the trees. Today, the walk had been so invigorating that she'd passed her farmhouse and taken a second path, which led to her fields on the far side of the farm. This section was sadly overgrown and made for difficult walking. After a few hundred yards, Lydia decided to turn around and go back to the stable path. As she swung around, a large shadow floated over the path then disappeared. It was the shadow of a man. A twig snapped. The sound had been close. Lydia froze and swallowed hard. Nervously, she glanced around. Was someone following her? She saw nothing but trees and leaves. Perhaps she was more tired than she had realized.

Whatever the case, she turned back again and continued to trek up to the fields. The terrain might be more difficult, but she was closer to that opening than to the stable. She walked on, increasing her pace. Again, there was movement behind her. Leaves crunched, more twigs snapped. Lydia sucked in a quick breath. She paused and listened. Were those footsteps she heard? She wasn't sure but something was behind her. She could sense it. *Oh dear Lord, let me find my way home.*

FOUR

At his workstation, Joseph found a folded note that had been placed next to his tools. Someone must have left it there while he was chatting with Bishop Miller. He opened it and read the computer-printed message.

If you're smart you'll disappear back to Indiana and take your girlfriend with you. If you're not smart, I'll help you both disappear.

Joseph searched the work space. Only one other craftsman remained this late on a Friday afternoon.

"Did you see anyone come in?" Joseph asked him.

The man shook his head. He was busy sanding, which was noisy. So someone could have slipped in through the back doors, which were open for ventilation, left a note for him then slipped back out unseen.

Joseph read the message again. Girlfriend? Could it mean Lydia?

Lydia, who'd gone home alone through the woods. His heart began to pound. He didn't waste a second. He was probably overreacting but he wasn't taking any chances. He ran out the back, around to the parking lot and across the street then tore down the old footpath that Lydia had taken.

By now, she should have reached the farmhouse or at least her stable. But he called to her anyway. There was no answer. But he could see her footprints in the muddy path.

He reached the creek—the halfway point—and crossed. The mud was thicker on this side, but strangely Lydia had left no prints. The path was clean. It was as if she had disappeared. Shock and panic pumped through Joseph's veins. He hurried on, calling her name with every other step.

Running hard, he reached the farm quickly. The stable was just ahead. He scanned the open area, panting, his leg muscles aching with lactic acid. "Lydia…Lydia."

A couple of miniature ponies lifted their heads from the grass, then, seeing it was him, went back to their grazing. Joseph checked toward the house. No one. Could she still be in those woods? An uneasy feeling took hold of him. The words *make you disappear* in the message were ever present in his frantic mind.

Joseph paced the edge of the forest. He could go back in and try to find the spot where her footprints had ended. But by that time she could be even farther away. He hated the thought. Once again, Joseph scanned the fields and gardens around the farmhouse and the stable, calling for Lydia. Finally, he saw movement at the house, but before he sighed with relief, he realized that it wasn't Lydia but Naomi Stoltz running out to join him.

Naomi wiped her hands on her apron as she hurried toward him. "Joseph, what is it? Where is Lydia?"

"Lydia's not in the house?"

Naomi shook her head.

"I should have passed her on the path through the woods. She should be home. She left the store a while ago. I think she's still in the woods."

"You seem worried."

"I am. She should have been home by now." He thought it best not to mention the threatening note at this time.

"Go look for her, Joseph," she said. "I'll ring the bell and call for help."

Mrs. Stoltz fled to the big bell in the front of the farmhouse. Whenever anyone in the Amish community rang a bell, neighbors knew someone needed a hand. Friends would come from all over. It was the Amish call for assistance. Joseph rushed back to the edge of the woods, searching and praying. *Please, Lord, let the bell call her home.*

Benjamin Zook and his three burley sons rolled up to the farmhouse in their open wagon only minutes after the bell sounded. They must have been close by the hill on the main road. When Joseph saw them, he ran across the far fields to the other side of the woods. Maybe she had missed the path at the creek and gone on to the fields…maybe…

Lydia's legs churned as fast as she could make them. Uphill. The wet leaves and muddy earth made for slick ground. She slipped and struggled to make her way. It seemed that whatever was behind her was only getting closer and closer. Nervously, she looked back.

He was there. A dark figure. A man. He wore black

clothing and a dark cap, which shaded the whole of his face. Like a ghost, he vanished behind a tree.

Sharp tremors rattled her. She could not ignore what all her senses were telling her. Someone was there. She'd been foolish to stop. Each time, he had only moved closer.

As fast as she could, Lydia ran up the second half of the hill. But his footsteps were close. Gaining. At last, she rounded the peak and finally she saw a break in the thick of forest trees.

If only she could make it out into the open. *Please, Lord...*

Lydia had barely started her prayer when a bell sounded. Like manna from heaven, she followed the sweet ringing over the ridge of the hill and into a small clearing. She was almost home.

"Lydia! Lih-dee-yah!" Her name echoed across the enclosure. It was Joseph.

Lydia's figure appeared at the far west end of her property. She scrambled out of the woods at an alarming speed. Her blond locks fell loose around her face, which was twisted with fear. Her white apron had bits of leaves and mud from the forest. She glanced more than once over her shoulder before running into his arms.

"Thank God, you are safe." He pulled her tight to his chest.

"Someone...someone was chasing me." She trembled.

"Someone was following you? Did you see who it was?" He wiped the tears from her face with his thumb.

"No, I couldn't see his face. But he was big. It had to be a man. Oh, Joseph, I was so scared…"

"Shh. It's okay now. You're okay." Joseph scanned the edges of the forest at the spot where she'd come out. He didn't see any movement. Of course, with a loud bell ringing out across the countryside, even a fool would know he'd better run in the other direction.

For a long moment, Joseph held on to Lydia, drinking in the feel of her weight against his shoulder. He had forgotten how nicely she fit against him. How good she smelled. Then she pulled away and he remembered the note and Billy's death. And he remembered how Lydia had forgotten him the second he'd gone to Indiana.

He patted her shoulder. "Let's go back to the house. Your mother is so worried. We'll get you cleaned up and warm again. And we'll need to call Detective Macy. Someone left us a threatening note."

Joseph didn't spend any more time with Lydia that evening. Her mother hovered over her, then Detective Macy arrived. By that time, Lydia was tired and had begun to downplay her fears and suspicions.

The police searched the woods, but they quickly had business to attend to elsewhere, which took precedence. Detective Macy left them, saying he would up the number of patrol cars that passed by and that he thought no one should be out traveling alone.

Mr. Zook instructed his three sons to sleep in the Stoltz's living room that night and offered Joseph a ride back to his parents' place. He left disappointed, worried and confused. He was not looking forward to Billy's funeral, which was merely hours away.

* * *

Early the next morning, Joseph drove Cherry, his chestnut Morgan, once again up Holly Hill to the Stoltz's quaint farmhouse. The sun peeked across the eastern sky, casting pale light over the lush green fields framed by the white fencing and bright gray stones. Lydia waited, leaning against a wooden post on the front porch, slender and petite like a china doll. Her pink lips and dark eyes offered the only contrast to her milky skin.

It would be a long journey to the church where Billy's funeral was to be held. Like him, she'd probably been up for hours, tending to her animals. Of course, there were no traces of farm on her now. She was dressed in a fine frock, with a crisp white apron pinned over top. Her dark blond hair had been parted down the middle, brushed smooth then twisted in a bun and tucked under a white prayer *kapp,* which concealed from the world most of its beauty. Joseph, however, could easily imagine her locks reached far down her back and still held the same wavy curls they had when she was a girl.

"It's a fine day for a long buggy ride." He slowed the vehicle at the end of the front walk. She floated down the stairs and helped herself into the buggy before he could get out and assist her like a proper gentleman.

"I thank ye for offering a ride. The Zook boys were kind enough to take care of my chores this morning." She folded her hands neatly in her lap, sat tall and looked straight ahead.

Joseph clicked to Cherry. The mare took off at a nice steady trot. "How are things at the farm?"

"Fine."

"Fine?" Joseph said. "That's not what I hear."

Lydia stiffened. "What do you hear?"

"I heard that you and your *mamm* were running things better than any of the Stoltz men could have ever dreamed."

"I don't like being compared to my *dat*."

Lydia didn't like anyone mentioning her *dat*. As close as they'd been, she'd never opened up to him about her father and why he'd left. He supposed now she never would. "So, I didn't really get to speak to you last night. What did Macy have to say?"

She shrugged. "He asked a lot more questions. Frankly, it was all a bit overwhelming. What did he say to you?"

"I gave him the note that I told you about. He didn't say much about it. I thought he would. Then again, the more I think on all this, the less sense it makes."

"How can anyone make sense of murder?"

"True." Joseph shifted positions. "Macy asked me again about the old days."

Lydia exhaled a sharp breath. "*Ya,* me, too. But I had nothing to say. Like my mother said, the past is passed."

Joseph knew that her words extended beyond the situation with Billy Ferris. She meant that she didn't want to talk about their past, either. But he might not let her off so easy. After seeing her again, he wanted some answers. He wanted to know why—no, how she'd let go of everything without any explanation. Why didn't she read his letters or write back to him? "Today might not be the day, Lydia. But we will talk about the past. Our past. I think we must."

Lydia nearly turned her back to him. "It will change nothing. What's done is done."

Joseph saw no reason to press her. There was already so much emotion in the air. "Did Macy tell you about the red Camaro?"

"A car? No, I didn't hear about that."

"Billy drove a red sports car. The police found it abandoned in the woods near Miller's store. Billy's blood was in the car and so was the murder weapon, a hunting knife. But there were no prints. Whoever killed Billy wiped the car clean."

Slowly, Lydia looked his way. "How near?"

"Near enough that the store was in view."

Lydia narrowed her eyes on him. "What are you not telling me?"

Joseph took a deep breath. "The police think that Billy knew who attacked him. They think it was someone he trusted and possibly allowed into his car."

"But once this person attacked Billy, why would he let him get away and go to Miller's store?"

"I asked the same question," Joseph said. "Macy thinks it could be one of two possibilities. Billy could have hurt his attacker and got away. He did have a gun in his hands. Although forensic testing showed it had not been fired."

"What's the other possibility?"

"The killer allowed Billy to leave. He wanted to see where Billy would go. Maybe he followed him to the store to see who he would talk to. Or he sent Billy to us with a message on purpose."

"That would mean we *are* somehow involved."

"*Ya.* Well, at this point, it seems we are, no?"

"What do you think?"

"I think Billy knew the killer, got away from him and came to us with or without a real message. Then the killer probably followed him, and in that case, he knows Billy talked to us before he died."

"But Billy didn't tell us anything."

"No, he didn't. But the killer doesn't know that."

FIVE

Joseph pulled the buggy into the parking lot of Lancaster First Community Church. It was time to pay respects to an old friend.

Joseph recognized many faces at the small gathering, including Billy's family. Kind words were shared about the playful and happy side that Billy often showed to others. His father and his little sister, Anna, spoke about their memories of Billy. At the end of the service, Anna played a five-minute video slide show of Billy with family and friends over the years. Joseph was surprised to find himself in three or four of the photos that shone on the big white screen at the front of the church.

Thou shalt not make unto thee any graven image... Joseph recalled the verse from Exodus, which many Amish brethren held to the letter. His shame in being photographed was a sharp reminder of the many careless decisions of his youth.

Joseph was thankful for a forgiving God.

After the service, Billy's father made a point to speak to them. Joseph supposed they were pretty easy to spot in the crowd because of their plain dress.

"It's been a long time." Mr. Ferris gave Joseph's hand

a hearty shake and nodded to Lydia. "You look well. Indiana air must agree with you."

"*Ya,* I suppose so...." He cast a furtive glance at Lydia. "I'm very sorry about what happened to your son."

"I understand you were with him just before he died." Mr. Ferris struggled with his words. "Did—did he suffer greatly?"

"I'm sorry, Mr. Ferris," Joseph said. "I'm afraid he suffered a great deal. But I don't know how conscious he was. I'm sorry we could not have done more." *I'm sorry we couldn't save him.* But it was not the Lord's will.

"He was with people who loved him. I'm thankful for that....Come. I have something for you." Mr. Ferris motioned for them to follow. They cut through the center of the sanctuary to a private room that had been stocked with pastries and other things for the mourning family members. He offered them coffee and biscuits, which they declined. Then he retrieved a small wooden box from a bag in the corner. It was quite plain, made of maple and opened with a simple pin hinge. Joseph recognized it immediately.

"I made that for Billy." He smiled. To see the piece again after all these years brought him a sense of sweet nostalgia. "It's a valet box, one of my first pieces."

Mr. Ferris placed the box in his hands. "Billy moved out a few years ago, but he left this behind. He said he didn't want anything to happen to it because one day he would give it back to you so that...well, so that you would remember the old days."

"Did he?" Joseph nodded, turning the little container over in his hands.

"Billy bought many of your pieces online. Had them shipped all the way from Indiana. Your tables are in the restaurant. He admired them so. He was very proud of you…loved you like a brother."

"And I loved him. Thank you for this." Joseph raised the small box. "This means a lot."

Mr. Ferris gave Joseph's shoulder a firm touch then turned back to face the crowd awaiting him at the front of the church.

Lydia could see the tears building in the corners of Joseph's eyes. He was struggling. As was she. The past few days had dredged up so many difficult memories and emotions. Right now, Lydia just wanted to get back to the farm and be with her animals, where she felt more in control of things. She pressed her way through the lines of people waiting to see Billy's family. Joseph struggled to keep up.

"Slow down." He got close enough to reach her shoulder from behind. "There's no fire."

Lydia cut her eyes toward the warm, strong hand resting on her shoulder. She glanced behind at Joseph. "Okay, slower."

But now she couldn't move at all. A large man had blocked the exit. It was all she could do not to barrel straight into him.

"Excuse me." She stepped back, embarrassed. It was Mr. Bowman, the restaurant owner who'd come to the shop the day before.

"Hello." He wore a fine wool suit, one of the fanciest Lydia had ever seen. He looked straight at Joseph. "Aren't you Jason? You used to wash dishes with Billy, right?"

Joseph gave Lydia's shoulder another squeeze. It must have been quite obvious how uncomfortable and upset she was.

"Mr. Bowman." Joseph shook the man's hand. "Actually...I'm Joseph and this is Lydia. And yes, yes, I did work for you."

"Of course, Joseph and Lydia." He stared at the wooden box in Joseph's hands. Lydia could see the top of his shiny bald head. Slowly, she tried to scoot away, but another, younger man came and flanked her on the left.

"I understand you were with Billy at Miller's store the night he died," Bowman said.

"Yes, sir." Joseph tipped his head in an abbreviated nod.

"So sad." Bowman's words were flat and rehearsed. "Ferris sure knew how to run that restaurant. Kevin here will have some pretty big shoes to fill." He motioned to the man on the other side of Lydia.

"Hi. Kevin Watson." The young man shook both their hands. Lydia noticed that, he, too eyed the small valet box, which Joseph kept in his left hand. "I worked with Billy for years at the restaurant. Please come by. Have dinner on the house."

"Thank you. That's a kind offer. But for now we must be off." Much to Lydia's relief, Joseph tipped his black felt hat and turned to leave. Grabbing her hand, he led her through the exit. Apparently, Joseph wanted out of there as badly as she did. As they hurried off, Lydia couldn't shake the sensation that Mr. Bowman and Mr. Watson were watching them. It gave her an uneasy feeling, but she resisted the temptation to turn around and see if her assumption was correct.

Soon, the clip-clop of the horse's trot steadied Lydia's unbalanced emotions. She prayed silently for her own strength to get past this tragedy and the memories it had stirred.

It didn't help, either, that the more time she was in the presence of Joseph Yoder the more difficult it became to ignore her attraction to him and his changes—this new calmness and maturity that he now possessed. She supposed it was only natural that he'd grown up at some point. Then again, she reminded herself that even maturity didn't make up for his leaving her.

Joseph whistled to his mare to pick up speed. "I guess I didn't realize that Billy was still working for Mr. Bowman."

"He startled me. I had not seen him there. I guess he came in after it started."

"I saw him. He was in the back playing with his cell phone though most of the service."

"How rude. Why even bother coming? I know it sounds like I am judging but he did sound so phony yesterday when he came to the store to order more furniture. I think he just wanted to see where Billy had died. It may be wrong to say so but he gives me the creeps."

"*Ya,* that's why I quit my job at the Amish Smorgasbord. Remember? Billy and I were dishwashers there a few nights a week. Good tips."

"I remember. Even then, Mr. Bowman would tell us to eat lunch for free." Lydia gave a half laugh. "Like any of us would want to eat *that* food. I'm afraid the only thing Amish about that restaurant is the name."

"And apparently, the tables." Joseph gave a teasing grin. They both had a laugh, which felt good and natural. But as quickly as the connection was made and felt, they fell into an awkward silence.

After a few minutes, Lydia picked up the valet box that Mr. Ferris had given to Joseph. She studied the plain style of it, then stopped as she felt Joseph's gaze on her hands. "Oh, I'm sorry. I should have asked. Do you mind if I look it over?"

"No, please." He smiled. "Open it."

Despite the cool autumn air against her cheeks, Lydia blushed. She turned the box over and studied the rounded edges and clean lines. "It is very sturdy. Perhaps you remember that you made one for me, as well."

"Of course I remember. I made yours first and I spent a lot more time on it." If Lydia didn't know better she would have said there was a hint of pride on his smiling face.

"It keeps all my sewing needles, scissors and thread. It is very useful." Usefulness was the highest compliment she could give his work. Saying it was beautiful or better than another's would sound like praise, and praise was something the Amish did not indulge in for fear of truly becoming proud.

Lydia unlocked the pin in front and opened the lid of the maple box. The insides were rough and unfinished. "It's empty."

"Were you expecting something?" he teased her. "A golden treasure or jewels perhaps?"

"Don't be silly, Joseph Yoder," she protested. "It just seems a shame that something so suitable was given no purpose."

A large sky-blue pickup truck had dashed around and in front of them, then slammed on its brakes to make a left turn. Tires screeched across the road. A blur of blue swirled around Lydia.

"Whoa." Joseph pulled back hard on the reins.

The truck had allowed almost no space between it and the chestnut mare, which was traveling along at a nice clip.

Cherry broke her gait and pressed down hard to slow herself and the buggy. Her metal shoes slid on the slick, oily asphalt. Joseph applied the hydraulic brakes, common in a buggy of such size. But nothing seemed to slow their forward momentum.

Joseph's eyes went wide. He pumped the pedal again and again. The buggy was not slowing down and all of its weight pressed against the backside of the poor mare.

"The brakes are gone." Joseph stretched an arm across in front of Lydia hoping to keep her from slamming into the windshield, but she was just out of his reach.

Lydia braced for the crash. At the same time, the mare turned to the side to avoid crashing into the truck. The buggy, of course, turned, too. The torque pulled Lydia from her seat. Lydia felt herself slipping.

Joseph reached again for her. The tips of his fingers caught the sleeve of her frock. But it was not enough to hold her in. The thin garment pulled from his grasp. And the momentum of the turn threw Lydia from the vehicle.

* * *

The buggy jolted, tipped as it turned, then landed back on all four wheels. It was still settling when Joseph leaped from his seat and ran to where Lydia lay on the asphalt. "Are you okay? Lydia? Lydia?"

Lydia did not move. She lay lifeless in the middle of the highway, face up, eyes closed. The valet box was smashed to pieces on the street beside her.

An unrelenting tightness grabbed hold of Joseph's lungs. His heart seemed to stop. He couldn't breathe but he didn't care. The only thing that mattered was Lydia.

"Please, someone call 911." Joseph sensed other cars had stopped around his buggy along the side of the highway. Someone was holding Cherry by the reins. Another person shouted they had a cell phone. Another said they'd written down the license-plate numbers of the truck that had cut in front of them.

Joseph knelt and scooped Lydia's head and shoulders into his arms and held her close. She was warm against his skin and he could feel her pulse, slow and steady at her throat. She did not wake. She did not respond. No matter how he stroked her cheek or whispered to her, she was limp in his arms.

Please, Lord. Please. Not Lydia. Please don't take Lydia...

Joseph only opened his eyes when two EMTs pulled Lydia from his embrace. He had no idea how much time had passed, but he didn't want to let go of her. As Joseph felt the separation, he realized what he had done. By going to Indiana, he had abandoned her just like her father. And for that, she would never forgive him.

SIX

Lydia awoke to familiar comforts—the smell of her mother's yeast rolls rising in the oven, the softness of their old blue couch underneath her and the sound of Joseph's voice. Her eyes flickered open. His handsome face broke into a smile over her.

"Look who's back among the living." His announcement grabbed the attention of her mother, who ran over from the kitchen and planted a kiss on the forehead.

"What happened? Last thing I remember we were on our way home from the funeral."

Joseph helped her up into a sitting position. As she rose, a throbbing in the back of her head shot across her skull. She remembered the blue truck and Joseph reaching for her.

"You were thrown from the buggy."

"Ya." She rubbed the bump on the back of her head. "A truck pulled in front of us. I slipped from the buggy. The rest of it I don't remember. How did we get here?"

"The emergency crew brought us. Detective Macy and a whole team of police came to the scene. I told them about the brakes not working. They are looking into it. Inspecting the buggy. A man came with a horse trailer and took Cherry back to my parents' place."

"I'm so thankful you are okay," her mother said before heading back to the stove. By the warm, delicious smells floating through the air, Lydia guessed her mother had baked quite a dinner. She must have been sleeping for hours.

"How do you feel?" Joseph asked.

"My stomach's growling. I'm thinking that's a good sign." She invited him to sit beside her. The concerned look in his eyes warmed her from head to toe. Yesterday, she would not have welcomed it. *Be careful, Lydia,* she warned herself.

"You gave me quite a scare, Miss Stoltz. Two days in a row. You have to stop doing this to me." He took her hand in his own. He held tightly to her. Lydia filled with emotion at the tenderness of his touch. Her cheeks felt warm. "Macy will be here soon to talk to us again. Are you up for that?"

She nodded. "I think so. Really I just have a bit of headache. I'm sure I'll feel fine as soon as I eat."

His soft hazel eyes held her gaze for a long moment. Her pulse raced as she saw in him that boy who'd loved her so. It would be easy to fall for him all over again. But she couldn't. He'd had his chance and he'd made his choice. She turned her head away. "So, when do you go back to Indiana?"

Joseph's expression darkened and he sighed. "You know very well I'm staying for my cousin's wedding. That's not for three weeks. Anyway, I can't go anywhere until Macy gives his permission, and I'm guessing that won't be until this mess with Billy is resolved."

"Right, I'm sorry. I suppose I'm not thinking straight after the bump on the head.... But I think I could use a cup of tea. You?" Lydia began to stand.

"You stay put. I'll go." Joseph grabbed her arm and kept her down.

While he fetched the tea, Detective Macy and another officer knocked at the front door. Her mother led them into the modest living area, where they each took a seat in a plain wooden chair.

"I hope you're feeling better, Miss Stoltz." Macy's voice and expression, which had always been stern and serious, seemed even more ominous.

Joseph returned with a large mug of hot tea for her. He greeted the officers and set the tea beside her.

"I'll go pour two more cups," her mother said.

"That won't be necessary." Detective Macy shook his head. "We won't stay long." He turned to the man who'd accompanied him. "This is Detective Mason. He inspected your vehicle, Mr. Yoder."

"How's the buggy?" Joseph asked.

"It's a little bumped up, but the biggest concern is the brakes. When was the last time you remember using them?" Detective Mason asked him.

"They didn't work at the accident, but I'm certain that they worked earlier. I'd used them on the ride out to the church. They seemed fine. What happened?"

Macy and Mason exchanged a serious look. "It seems someone removed your entire brake system. It wasn't that they didn't work. You didn't have any. If you remember using them earlier today, then the removal must have been done during the service."

"Why would anyone do that?" Lydia felt her eyes go wide.

"We don't know. Perhaps in hopes that you or Joseph or both of you would be injured. Detained. Scared. Killed." Detective Macy handed Joseph a small envelope.

"What's this?" Joseph took it.

"One of the witnesses to the accident picked up a couple of things that had blown out of Lydia's hands."

"Oh no." Lydia remembered the valet box had been in her hands as she fell. "The box broke. I'm sorry, Joseph. It was all you had from Billy."

Joseph turned his head toward her. "If that's all that was damaged, then I have everything to be thankful for. God's hand was truly on us."

"Amen," her mother added.

Lydia studied the small envelope Joseph held. "So, there must have been something inside the valet box after all."

"*Ya.* Perhaps tucked up in the lid." Joseph placed the envelope on the sofa. "Let's look at it later. I want to hear more about the accident." He turned back to Detective Macy. "What about the truck that tried to run us off the road? Were you able to locate it?"

"No. Those plate numbers were phony. The truck could be stolen. We won't be able to trace it."

With that, Macy stood and Detective Mason followed his example.

"I'm going to increase the amount of patrol cars circling around here," Macy continued. "I think the two of you should continue to play it safe. Stay in numbers. Don't go anywhere alone.

"With your brakes having been removed, we cannot write off this accident as coincidence. I think we must assume that someone or some group of people wish to harm you. A logical conclusion is that it is connected to Billy Ferris's death. Possibly someone—maybe a killer—knows that Billy went to talk to you both after he was injured. He or she may think that Billy gave you something of value or told you something that could incriminate him.

"If you think of anything, let me know...especially if you can remember exactly what Billy said to you before he died. Please call. I'll be in touch soon."

Joseph stood to see the officers out, then sat beside her again, picking up the envelope and holding it in his hand. "You know, Macy is right. We both knew that Billy said to be careful. Well, that accident scared me enough to think we'd better find out why. I've already talked it over with your mother and sent word to my family. I'll be staying here with you and your *mamm* for a few days. That way I can help out with the farm, since you need to rest that head. And I won't have to worry about you two women out here on this isolated farm by yourselves."

He studied her, obviously trying to gauge her feelings, but she made sure her face showed neither happiness nor discontentment. Anyway, it wasn't far from the truth. She wasn't sure how she felt about Joseph staying so close.

He lifted the envelope and took out the contents. "Pictures? Let's take a look."

He handed her what he had pulled from the envelope.

Lydia smiled, taking the photos and separating them in her hands. "There are two. Billy is in both of them."

In the first, Billy had his arm around the shoulders of another guy in a pal-like sort of way. The other boy was tall, like Billy, and they both had long hair.

"I don't think I know this guy." Joseph leaned in to study the photo more closely. "This one looks like it was taken when Billy was in high school."

Lydia turned to the second photo but quickly dropped it away from her face. This was not a picture she wanted to see. Her stomach churned.

"What? What is it?" He reached across her lap for the second picture.

"It's nothing, Joseph. Just so many memories all at once…"

He touched her hand, lifting the photo up again so that he could see it. "Oh…yeah…this must have been taken that last night when we were all together…at Tucker's Pond. All those girls were sitting together in our—in my old courtin' buggy."

She handed the second picture to him. A small piece of paper slipped from the back of the photo and fluttered to the floor. Lydia bent over to retrieve it, then she held it between them so that they could read the words together.

And you shall know the truth, and the truth shall make you free.

"A Scripture from John. Maybe it was his favorite verse?" Lydia said.

"I don't think so."

"Why not?"

"Billy wasn't too into the Bible. I'm thinking he meant something by having it stuck to the back of this photo." Joseph turned the photos over in his hands. A deep frown darkened his face. The pictures, the memories of what had passed that night, obviously affected him, too.

"Put these back in the envelope, please." He handed the pictures back to her.

"Why does everything keep going back to that night?" Joseph stood and paced the length of the room. His frustration growing, he felt powerless, caught in this mess Billy had pulled them into. "I know you don't want to talk about the past, but I'm going to say this anyway. I hate that night. Lydia, I hate it. I exposed you to evil. I should have protected you. I should have taken better care of you. I was so stupid back then. So childish and naive. I never thought about the ripple effects of my decisions. But that night scared me.

"When that girl got sick, after I got you home, I told my parents that they were right. That I needed to get away from Billy. Away from his influence. They were more than happy to hear it. They didn't waste any time. My *daed* set me off the next morning to Indiana. They said it was best if I didn't see you first. They were afraid I'd change my mind. I had planned to come back after a year. To join the church here and be with you but you'd taken up with Gideon and my uncle needed me. I wish you'd read my letters."

"I was childish, too. And hurt." A sad smile passed

over her lips. "Anyway, so much time has passed. It is all forgotten."

"No, not all of it is forgotten…." He leaned close to her and again touched her hand. How he hoped she would not pull it away. "Lydia, surely not all of what we shared is forgotten. When you spend so much time with someone, doesn't that person become—"

Lydia's face washed white with his words. Joseph dropped his head. What was he thinking bringing this up now? She had a head injury, poor thing.

Anyway, there was no future for them. Not together. She would never leave her mother alone with the farm and he'd promised his uncle to return to Indiana. He needed to be thankful for this time to repair their friendship, not keep pushing for something he couldn't have. Something that Lydia clearly did not want.

"Dinner!" Lydia's mother yelled from the kitchen.

Joseph gave thanks for the food and for God's saving them on the road that very afternoon. Then dinner passed quietly.

Lydia ate little and spoke even less. She and her mother discussed the accident and the warning from Detective Macy. Joseph couldn't get his mind off the photos and the Bible verse. What had Billy meant by leaving them in the valet box for him? Could it possibly have anything to do with who killed him?

"I wonder what happened to the people in the photos that were inside the valet box. Do you remember any of them?" he asked.

"No." Lydia shook her head.

"What if we could find out what happened to them? Maybe we could ask them about what happened after we left that night. Or maybe they know something about Billy that would be helpful to us. Maybe then we could figure out if any of this really has to do with us."

"We'd have to remember their names for that," Lydia pointed out.

"Were they all students at Willow Trace High with Billy?" her mother said.

"I believe so. Why?"

"Because then you can look through the school's yearbooks for the years that Billy was in high school. You're bound to find at least one picture of each of them."

Joseph smiled. "When does the library open?"

SEVEN

Monday morning after chores, Lydia and her mother drove up the main highway in their pony cart. A bright yellow sun warmed their faces. A thick wool blanket kept their legs warm. Joseph had left earlier for Miller's shop to work. The bishop himself had stopped by to escort him and to check on everyone. Her mother had some shopping to do, while Lydia planned to meet Joseph at the library. They hoped that there they might learn something about the people in Billy's photos. And from that, they hoped to find out why Billy had come to them that night he died.

"I didn't want you to go to town alone," Lydia's mother said, turning toward her. "But I came along for another reason."

Oh boy. Advice in the pony cart. Her mother hadn't pulled this trick on her since her *rumspringa* days.

"You want to talk?" Lydia smiled.

"I do," her mother said. "Lydia…"

A long moment passed and her mother had yet to begin. "What is it, Mamm?"

"Well, this is harder than I thought." Naomi wiped a tear from her cheek. "I'm worried about you, Lydia."

"Why? From that little bump on the head? Don't. I'm fine."

"No, it's not the head. It's not even this tragedy about Billy Ferris. It's just you. Lydia, you aren't fine. You work too hard. You hardly ever spend time with your girlfriends, Kate and Miriam. You haven't been to a quilting in I don't know when. You cringe every time someone mentions the word *marriage*."

"That's not so." Lydia kept the smile on her face even though her mother's harsh accusations hurt. Every word her mother said was true. "Kate and Miriam don't have much time for me now that they're married. And the last few times I visited Kate, she could not stop talking about her time coming with the baby. I didn't know what to say. I certainly don't cringe when marriage is mentioned. I have nothing against marriage. I'm just all nervous about this business with Billy Ferris."

"This has nothing to do with Billy Ferris and you know it. I'm talking about why you aren't courting. You've had plenty of callers, but you keep turning them away. They've all but quit coming. They're afraid of getting rejected."

"You don't want me to get married to just anyone, do you? I have to wait for the right man."

"Your being choosy has nothing to do with it." Her mother's voice had taken an angrier, disappointed tone.

Lydia had not fooled Naomi with the phony smile and silly explanations. She frowned as she mulled over her mother's words. "I don't know why I don't get out much anymore. I'm older than most of the girls at the barn singings. There is a lot of work to do on the farm. But I'll make a better effort, Mamm. I will. Anyway, how can you bring that up with all of this horrible Billy Ferris business?"

"Because this Billy Ferris business is what made me realize what I've allowed you to get away with for the past few years." Her mother frowned. "And I've realized why you gave up on courting and love and men."

Lydia swallowed hard. "I didn't give it up. I—"

"First of all, you're afraid of men because your father upped and left us. Darling Lydia, your father is— was—a good man, but the Amish life was hard for him. He left us because he wasn't able to cope with the Amish ways. I pray every day that he is safe and happy. Maybe he will come home one day. Maybe he won't. But I will never judge another human based on his weaknesses and shortcomings."

"Did you want to go with Daed when he left?"

Naomi shook her head slowly. "I miss him, but my first vow is to God. I never had a doubt about that."

Lydia sighed. She did not understand her mother's complacency. "You aren't angry? You don't feel like you got a raw deal?"

Naomi shook her head and smiled. "How can I be angry about a relationship that gave you to me?"

"You're so forgiving, Mamm. I am not like you. I try but—"

"It's fear that keeps you from letting go of all this pain. The Scripture says that "you shall not be afraid." Try it, Lydia. Cast away the fear, and then the forgiveness and the love will come. And with that, you will have peace."

Lydia hoped one day to be the strong woman of

God that her mother was. "*Danki.* I will try. I will try harder."

"Wait. I'm not finished."

"You're not?" Lydia sank down in her seat.

"No, and I think you know what I'm going to say." Her mother eyed her with a knowing stare.

"Actually, I don't."

"Lydia, you are still in love with Joseph Yoder," her mother said.

"No, It is good to see him again and repair that childhood friendship. But I'm not in love with him."

She put her arm around Lydia's shoulders and pulled her near. "Take care, Lydia, that you do not lose something that could bring you joy and happiness in this life. There is so much God has for you. Don't be afraid of it."

Lydia could hardly breathe at the thought of losing the farm or leaving her mother. And Joseph she had already lost. As soon as he could, he would be going back to Indiana. Even if she did still love him, there was nothing good to come of it.

Her mother remained quiet for the rest of the ride into town, and Lydia tried hard not to dwell on their conversation. But it kept replaying in her mind. She was grateful when they pulled up to the library.

Joseph was waiting for her. She climbed out of the cart and gave her mother a kiss goodbye. Her *mamm* had certainly given her a lot to think about. But first to find out about Billy and his friends.

Joseph leaned over Lydia's shoulder, passing her the Willow Trace High School yearbooks he'd pulled from the shelves. It was nice to be so close that he could feel the warmth radiating from her skin. He liked being with Lydia. Staying with her over the past two days, sleeping on her couch, driving her and her *mamm* to Sunday meeting, taking meals with them, it had renewed and repaired their friendship.

If only the shadow of Billy's murder didn't hover over them constantly... Joseph really hoped they would find something useful that they could pass on to Detective Macy. He was ready to get them out of harm's way. He was also ready to really talk to Lydia about her feelings.

"What should we do first?" He whispered low and close to her ear even though they seemed to be the only patrons in the library.

"First, I think we should find the names of Billy's friends who are in those photos." She handed him a couple of annuals. "Here. You take these two. I'll take the others and that will cover all four years Billy was at Willow High."

Joseph took his two volumes and sat across the broad wooden table from Lydia. Several minutes passed while they flipped through page after page in the yearbooks. Joseph split his attention equally between the photo scanning and staring across the table at Lydia. She was so beautiful, even more so now than when he'd left five years ago. There was more gold in her eyes. Her lips a darker shade of rose, her cheeks higher, more pronounced.

"What?" She looked up suddenly and caught him staring.

Joseph gave her a quick smile. Was this his chance to finish asking Lydia why her feelings for him had changed? He would have to ease into the subject. "I—I was just thinking…well, I'm surprised you're not married."

"*Ya,* I'm an old maid. *Danki.* My mother just said the same thing to me on the way here. Now, get back to the pictures."

Joseph dropped his head back to the yearbook. After he'd inspected about three more pages, Lydia swung her edition around to him.

"Look." She pointed at a class photo in the middle of the page. "This is Michelle. She was in the picture and at the pond that night."

"*Ya.* I think Billy and she were sort of together at one point."

"Maybe the others will be nearby."

Lydia marked the page, then they went back to searching the individual albums. Joseph almost immediately came across a picture of Billy in a baseball uniform. He was standing next to another boy dressed the same. This time he turned his yearbook around to share. "Look at this one. I'd almost forgotten that Billy played baseball. And that guy next to him—he worked at the restaurant with us."

"That's the same guy in the picture from the valet box. What's his name?" There was excitement and hope in Lydia's voice.

"You're right. I'm surprised I didn't recognize him. I guess after the accident I wasn't thinking too clearly." Joseph read the caption under the photo. "'Bill Ferris and Kevin 'Wats' Watson pitch Willow High's first ever no-hitter.'"

Kevin Watson?

"Oh, Lydia. Remember? Billy said 'what's' to us that night he died. Maybe Billy wasn't saying 'what' *w-h-a-t*." He thought out loud. "He was trying to say 'Wats' *W-a-t-s?* As in Kevin Watson, the guy that took over his job at the restaurant? Wasn't that the name of the new manager? The one we met at the funeral."

"It was. You're right. And you did say he looked familiar," Lydia agreed. "What do you remember about him?"

"Not much." Joseph shrugged. "He was a year or two younger than Billy and me. At the restaurant, he would tag along after Mr. Bowman. You know, trying to impress him. Billy, I remember, thought he was a pain."

"I don't remember him being at Tucker's Pond that night. Do you?"

"No." He turned the book back around to face himself on the tabletop.

"Wait." Lydia hurried around to his side of the table and touched a photo on the opposing page. "Look at that!"

He smiled up at her. "There are all the girls from Billy's photo. They're all at a baseball game."

Joseph moved his finger to the caption under the photo, his hand brushing against hers. A tingling sensation traveled up his arm. "'Cheering on the regional champions to their final victory—Michelle Adams, Kelly Newport and Alexandra Nivens.'"

"Alexandra! Alex!" Lydia fell into the chair beside him, shaking her head. "We didn't imagine Billy saying that name, Joseph. He really said it. And he was talking about this girl." Her voice quivered. "The girl who became sick from the drugs. The one we left. We have to find out what happened to her after we left."

"Why don't we use the computers now and see if we can find something on the internet about any of them… especially Alex?" Lydia said.

Joseph and Lydia both stood so fast they met each other face-to-face and toe-to-toe. Joseph froze. The proximity of her filled his senses. He breathed in her scent and felt the warmth of her breath. She was achingly close. He touched her soft face with his fingertips. "Oh, Lydia."

He was so close, Lydia held her breath. A strange and overwhelming energy filled her every fiber. Every word her mother had said in the pony cart screamed through her head. *Joseph is not your* daed…. *You shall not be afraid…. You're still in love with Joseph….*

Was she? Was she still in love with him? And was it only fear that had kept her from reading his letters? Was it fear that, right this moment, kept her from falling into his arms and telling him she'd been wrong.

Lydia lowered her head and stepped back, her heart pounding. With a quick step, she walked to the computers. Joseph followed at her heels. He placed his hand on her shoulder and whispered her name. The warmth of his hand flowed from the tips of his fingers down her back. She was moved, excited and scared. Too scared to turn and say what was in her heart. If she let Joseph in, even the tiniest bit, he might leave her again. And from that she would never recover.

She pulled away again. "Let's just find out what happened to Alex and this can all be over."

She chose the first computer station. Taped next to the big screen was a set of easy-to-follow steps for the Amish patrons and others who weren't familiar with the web searches. Lydia had used the internet a few times during her *rumspringa*. Without much difficulty, she opened the browser and typed in *Alexandra Nivens*.

"Wow. There must be a hundred articles with her name." Joseph pulled a chair up alongside her.

He was silent for the moment, but Lydia feared he would try again to speak of his feelings. But really, what was the point? He was going back to Indiana. She shook the troublesome thoughts from her head. They had to focus on Billy's death.

"I don't know why there are so many articles. Let's see." She scrolled down, reading aloud the titles. "'High School Student Goes Missing,' 'Last Seen,' 'Unsolved Case,' 'Missing Person,' 'Nivens Missing'..."

"Alexandra Nivens is a missing person."

EIGHT

Lydia clicked on one of the links to an article. He and Lydia began to skim the article silently, when he noticed the publication date.

"This is just a couple of days after that night at the pond. Here's a quote from Billy and Michelle. 'Last time we saw her was at school.'"

They exchanged a knowing glance. They both knew that wasn't true.

"School was out, wasn't it? The last time they would have seen her would have been at the pond with us. Or do I remember it all wrong?"

"No. You are right." Joseph touched his hand to his forehead. He swallowed hard. "That was the reason for the party. It was the last day of school. So Billy and Michelle lied to the newspaper."

"What would make them lie?"

"I don't know. Because of the drugs that night, maybe?"

Lydia couldn't quite wrap her head around the concept of lying, but she did not like where any of this was going. She turned back to the screen. "Here's another article. This one is from just last year."

"It's another missing-persons case from Lancaster," Joseph said, reading along with her. "A more recent one. Another teenage girl, Melissa. And two others in the year before following similar patterns. Look, it mentions Alexandra Nivens here... as an unsolved case."

He pointed to the screen. Lydia scrolled down, reading as fast as she could. "Alexandra has never been found, but read this."

Joseph followed her finger to the paragraph that she pointed out on the bright screen.

Melissa Roan was found dead three days after she went missing. Cause of death: overdose of designer drugs. Forensic scientists do not have enough evidence to trace the drugs to a particular dealer. Police profilers, however, suspect it is a local operation and are wondering if the Nivens missing-persons case and several others could be related to this crime. All girls fit similar description, age, size and situation.

"Come on," Joseph said quickly. "We have to get to Detective Macy and tell him that Billy tried to talk to us about Alex and Kevin the night he died."

Joseph stood and offered his hand to help her up. Until now, he had not seen her tears, but it was clear she had been crying as he'd read. Joseph held out his arms. Lydia stepped into his embrace and lowered her head to his shoulder. "I'm glad you have been here. I couldn't have gone through this without you."

Joseph's heart filled with emotion. He whispered into her ear and held her tight until she was calm again.

"I'm so sorry I took you there that night, Lydia. So sorry. This is all my fault. I got us involved in whatever this is. If I could, there are so many things I would have done differently in the past. And none of them would include hurting you."

He wasn't sure Lydia had heard a word of what he'd said, but her arms were tight around him and he wished they could stay like that forever.

Lydia and Joseph called Detective Macy from a public phone in the lobby of the library. It didn't take long to explain to him what they'd learned from the pictures and internet. The detective explained that Kevin Watson had already been on his radar for Billy's murder. Kevin had shown signs of distress and confusion when police had questioned him as a rival employee of Billy's. Upon further investigation, it was discovered that Watson had played a significant role in Billy's drug business, which he also coveted and wanted to take away from Billy. At that very moment there were police cars on their way to Kevin's home and to the restaurant to make an arrest. Macy promised to be in touch, but he hoped that this was the end of it.

Somehow, Lydia felt little relief at this discovery. Even as they walked home and heard the sirens whirring in the distance—the very ones on their way to the restaurant to arrest Kevin—it still felt unresolved. Kind of like her feelings for Joseph?

They had gone about a third of their hour to walk Holly Hill when Mr. Zook happened to pass them in his open buggy. He stopped to ask them about the sirens that had sounded earlier. When he realized they were walking all the way to Holly Hill, he insisted on giving them a ride. Joseph offered Lydia the bench seat next to Mr. Zook, but she preferred to stretch out in the cart and leave Joseph to answer all of Mr. Zook's questions.

Lydia must have been more exhausted than she thought. The next thing she knew, the buggy had stopped and she was home. She climbed down from with a yawn. Her mother was waving from the front porch.

"Thanks for the ride, Mr. Zook," she said, realizing Joseph was no longer with them.

"I let Joseph out at Miller's store." Mr. Zook must have sensed her confusion. "He said he had some business to take care of and that he wanted to update the bishop on the police making an arrest in Billy's murder."

She waved to Mr. Zook as he rode off in his open buggy and she walked up the steps to join her mother.

"Well, I'm glad to hear the whole affair is over. What a relief." Naomi put her arm around Lydia's shoulders and they moved toward the front door. "I fixed a ton of dinner. I thought Joseph would be with you. Where is he?"

Lydia shrugged. "Mr. Zook just told me he only rode to Miller's store. Said he had some business."

Her mother gave a doubting look. "Probably afraid you're going to send him back to Indiana without one kind word."

Lydia sighed. She was too tired to make a reply. She followed her mother to the kitchen and helped with the meal. "It does seem a bit quiet without Joseph or the Zook boys, doesn't it?"

Lydia ignored the strange emotions twisting inside of her. She also ignored her mother's I-told-you-so looks. She caught herself more than once peering out the kitchen window to see if Joseph was walking up the path.

The third time she peered out, she did see something moving. It wasn't Joseph. It was Candy, her larger pony, trotting down the gravel path. "Now, what is she doing out?"

"What's that?" her mother asked.

"Candy. She's gotten out of the stable. I'll be right back." Lydia hurried out of the house with an apple in her hand.

She ran down the front lane. A few whistles and the sweet fruit had the little pony at her side in no time. Lydia led Candy to the stable and locked her back inside her stall. How had she gotten out? Perhaps her mother had not shut the latch properly, but even then Candy would have had to slide the door to the stall. None of her ponies knew how to do that. Something wasn't right.

Lydia decided to check each of the ponies and the stalls. She tested the latches and made certain that the stalls were secure. She found nothing out of order. And yet, there was a nagging feeling that she had overlooked something.

Lydia marched back up the aisle once again, her eyes fixed on the feed room in the very back. The door had been left open—that was it. She headed over to the dark corner to pull it closed. Leaving the feed room open was the same as sending out party invitations to every unwanted critter in the vicinity. She couldn't imagine her mom had left it opened.

An empty bucket lay in front of the door. That, too, was strange. Her mother liked everything neat and orderly. A bad feeling washed over Lydia as she reached down and picked up the bucket from the dirt floor. Before she could stand again, a horse blanket came over her head and something or someone pressed her down to the ground. For a few seconds she tried to fight back and pull the blanket from her face. But her efforts were useless.

A second later, she took a hard blow to the head. Even with the cushion of the horse blanket, it sent pain ringing through her skull. Her limbs went limp. Darkness overtook her.

NINE

Joseph hummed a quick tune as he painted the last coat of stain across the top of a special piece of furniture he'd been working on. He'd started the chest when he'd first arrived in Willow Trace, thinking he could turn it over as a quick tourist item. But today, he'd decided to make it a gift to Lydia. He wasn't sure how he would present it to her. Just as he wasn't sure how he would ask for her forgiveness. But he had to try. And the chest wasn't the only reason he'd stopped at Miller's store. He'd wanted to talk to Bishop Miller about some major life choices. Afterward, they had prayed together and written to his uncle. The rest would be up to Lydia.

Joseph straightened up his workstation and headed out of the store toward Holly Hill. He had barely walked across the parking lot when Lydia's mother came running out of the woods.

"Joseph! Help, Joseph!" Naomi ran across the parking lot, waving her hands in the air. "She's gone. Lydia."

Joseph raced across the gravel lot to meet her. "What do mean, she's gone? Where?"

"I don't know. I don't know." Her voice cracked with emotion.

"It's okay, Mrs. Stoltz. It's okay. Tell me what happened."

"Lydia went out to catch Candy. The pony had gotten out. I saw her walk the pony back to the stable. But then she was gone for so long…"

"How long?"

She shook her head. "I don't know. But it was too long. I went outside to call her. And a van was driving away down the hill."

Gasping for air, Naomi's face twisted with grief and worry. "I didn't know what to do. I just started running here. Lydia said you were here."

"It's okay. It's okay, Mrs. Stoltz. We're going to find her." Joseph took Naomi's hands in his. She was hysterical, and even though he was close to feeling that way himself, he wanted her to tell him as much as she could. "Are you saying you think that Lydia went somewhere in a van? What van?"

"It was small. A little delivery van. White and gray. It was going so fast I couldn't see inside. I went to the stable as fast as I could…but I was too late. There was a huge mess in the aisles. Stuff everywhere. But Lydia was gone."

"A mess?" Joseph clenched his teeth. Lydia kept everything as neat as a pin. She would not have left the stable in disorder unless… "Someone took her."

Naomi covered her mouth. The tears slid down her cheeks. "I wouldn't have let her go outside alone, but I thought the murderer was caught. I thought this was all over."

"Me, too. We all thought it was over." Joseph put

an arm around Lydia's mother and steered her inside the shop.

"Bishop Miller?" He called out. "I think I'm going to need that prepaid cell phone you got the other day in case of an emergency."

Seconds later, the old bishop was running forward with his new phone in hand.

With trembling fingers, Joseph dialed Macy's direct number, which he remembered from the library. Macy answered on the first ring.

Joseph explained as quickly as possible what Naomi had told him.

"It's not Kevin Watson," Macy said over the line. "He is right here with me. But I think I know who it is. I'll send a patrol car for you. Where are you?"

"At the furniture store," Joseph said. "But why? Do you know where Lydia is? Who has her? Is she okay?"

"No, she's not okay. Maybe Bowman has her. I'll explain everything when I see you. But don't worry. Mr. Watson is going to cooperate and help us get Lydia back. Stay right where you are, Joseph."

"Hello? Hello?"

Macy had disconnected. Joseph looked at Bishop Miller and Mrs. Stoltz. What could he say that wouldn't send Naomi into the absolute frenzy that his mind was already in? "Detective Macy is sending a car over to pick us up. He says everything's going to be fine."

And Joseph prayed that it would. He prayed so hard.

Lydia came to with a start. One look around the smelly van she'd been thrown into and she knew it was a service truck. She tried to sit up but she had been bound at the wrists and ankles with heavy-duty plastic zip ties. The van traveled fast and made sharp turns. She fought in vain to keep upright, but mostly, she struggled to keep from hurting herself against the bread racks and other storage areas.

With some difficulty, she peeked through the small glass window between the front cab and the back of the van. Mr. Bowman, the restaurant owner, was at the wheel.

Lydia slid back against the side of the van. Mr. Bowman? What could he possibly want with her?

All afternoon, everyone had hoped the terror was over with the arrest of Kevin Watson. Did they have it all wrong? Lydia prayed and she prayed hard.

She should have been trembling. But for the first time in a long time, she felt peace. She thought of her mother, and of Joseph, and of all this time she'd closed herself off—afraid of her own feelings, afraid of loving again, afraid of being hurt. Tears of release spilled onto her cheeks.

Lydia lowered her head between her bound hands. *Whatever happens today, I have learned this lesson— I am not afraid. God, You have taken all my fear. And if I ever see Joseph again, I will tell him. I will tell him that I love him and that I'm not afraid. It won't matter if he loves me back or not.*

Lydia knew God would take care of her. Of course, she'd known it all along, but she hadn't felt it. She hadn't lived it. Her mother had been right. Her fears had stopped her. But no more.

Suddenly, the van came to a screeching halt. Mr. Bowman got out and walked around to the back.

"Hello again, pretty lady." He opened the back doors, grabbed her by the wrists and dragged her out of the vehicle.

Lydia hit the ground hard. And she knew exactly where she was. She'd been there five years ago on the worst night of her life. Tucker's Pond.

"Why have you brought me here? What do you want?"

"I want to get rid of you before you ruin everything. Just like Billy. Stupid ingrate. After all I did for him. I made him rich. He had girls. He made a fortune selling my drugs. He had anything he wanted." Bowman picked her up again, carried her to the edge of the pond and tossed her down in the grass.

"We thought it was Kevin who killed Billy. But all along it was you?"

"Kevin? That little twit would do anything I told him to. But he's a weakling. Good riddance. I thought he could be like Billy. But they all turn on you in the end."

"Why would you tell Kevin to kill Billy? What did Billy do to you?"

"He found out about my— Oh, stop with all of your stupid questions. You're giving me a headache. You'll figure it out soon enough." He turned back to the van. A moment later he came back with a bottle of water, a small brown lunch bag, and a set of large dumbbells and a rope.

Fear and darkness tried to surround her again. But Lydia fought it away. She looked up and faced him.

"You know Billy didn't tell us anything the night he died? You've been running around scaring us half to death for no reason at all. We don't know anything."

"For someone who doesn't know anything, you sure do talk a lot." He sat down on the ground next to her and pulled a plastic bag filled with powder from the brown sack. He paused for a quick moment and looked into her eyes. Lydia could see that same savage look that Billy had had the night he died. "You're going to feel so good, Amish girl," he said. "Just like the others. I made them feel so good. The first time wasn't planned, of course. Billy called me. Scared to death asking me what to do about Alexandra. He had made her sick with too much alcohol and one of those party drugs. I came here. I gave her something that made her feel all better. I loved watching her find that place of peace. My mother always told me when young girls were troubled, I should help them. Help end their suffering before they grow up. You're troubled, too, aren't you?"

"No. I am not troubled." Lydia jerked away from his hand that tried to stroke her on the wrist. "I'm perfectly fine."

"Now, you aren't telling the truth, young lady." He shook his head in a scolding manner. "I know your father left you. I know that Joseph Yoder left you. You might be the most troubled of them all. Well, don't worry. Today, I'll take all of that away." He touched her face and smiled. Them he poured the powder into the bottle of water and shook to mix it.

He was right. There was no mistaking his plan. His actions were rehearsed, memorized, habitual. He was going to drug her and send her to the bottom of the pond. He'd done it before. It sickened Lydia to think of it.

She turned away. If God willed her to be at the bottom of that pond, then so be it. It was only the flesh. Her spirit would live on. "I'm not afraid of you. You can't hurt me. But I do have a question."

"Another question? What's that?"

"If Billy knew all along that you killed Alexandra after the overdose, why did you wait to kill him five years later?"

"You're smarter than you look." He laughed. "Billy didn't know about Alexandra until a month ago. He thought I gave her a bunch of money and that she ran away from home. But then he found my—he found one of my keepsakes." He took the prayer *kapp* from her head. He held it gently in his hands. "Like this. From you, I will keep this. This is perfect."

"How many others, Mr. Bowman? How many women's lives did you steal?"

"I didn't steal their lives. I saved them."

"Only God can save."

"Drink the water." She had angered him to the edge now. He stood and forced the drugged water into her mouth.

Lydia turned and pressed herself facedown on the ground. It knocked the water from his hands.

He fumed. He grabbed the bottle from the grass, turned her over and forced the drink back to her lips. "You will drink this."

"I will not foul my body with your drugs, Mr. Bowman." She spit the drink from her mouth.

"You…" He lifted his hand to strike her but stopped. There was a sound in the distance.

A very familiar sound—a siren. Help was on the way! Lydia closed her eyes and thanked God.

Mr. Bowman cursed under his breath and, with one last look at her, turned and made a run for the van. He sped away, his tires spitting dirt and gravel back at her face. She watched as he drove like a madman to the far edge of the woods. A dark sedan pulled up and blocked his path. He slammed hard on his brakes then hopped out of his van and made a run for the woods. Lydia wanted to scream. But as if placed there by God's hands, Macy and his men came from behind the trees. They were on him and toppled him to the ground.

Joseph fled from the patrol car as soon as it stopped. Macy and his men had Mr. Bowman at the edge of the woods. But where was Lydia?

He ran to the back of the service van, but it was empty. Were they too late?

Joseph's eyes scanned the woods to the shoreline of the pond. At long last, he saw a blur of blue and white near the water. Lydia. She had worn a blue frock today.

Joseph ran to her as fast as his legs could go. He fell to his knees beside her at the water's edge. A bottle of water lay spilled out at her side. "Lydia, please be okay…"

She turned to his voice. A beautiful smile covered her face. "How did you know where to find me?"

"Kevin. He told Macy about it all. Billy had just found out, too. That's why—"

"I know. Mr. Bowman thought Billy told us, too."

Joseph nodded. He loosened the bindings around her hands and feet and tore them away. He pulled her up. His arms went around her waist and he hugged her close. It was perfect. She was perfect. He would never let go of her again. "It's all over now. We are safe."

"I don't want you to leave again, Joseph." She was crying and clung tight to his shoulders. "I want people to stay in my life. I want you to stay in my life, however that may be. I love you. I have always loved you. I was just afraid. But I'm not anymore. Can you forgive me for not reading your letters nor trying to understand why you left?"

He placed his hand on her chin and lifted her face to his. "If you can forgive me for leaving without talking to you first."

"I already have." She smiled. "I love you, Joseph. Even if you go back to Indiana, I will still love you."

"I love you, too." He leaned down and placed a soft kiss on her lips. "And I won't ever let go of you again, Lydia. That is, if you'll have me. Will you marry me, Lydia Stoltz?"

"Yes, yes, I will. I will marry you."

He kissed her forehead. He kissed her cheeks. He couldn't stop the huge smile that covered his face. But Lydia pulled away.

Her head dropped and the elated look from her eyes turned pensive and strained. Joseph's heart sank. Had she already changed her mind?

"I suppose we could sell the farm," she said.

"And why would you do that?" Joseph pressed his forehead against hers the way he used to do when they were young. He rubbed his nose against hers. "I want to stay here, don't you?"

"But I thought you had to—"

"No. It's all settled. I'm going to work for Bishop Miller."

Lydia looked fast into his eyes, as if she could not believe his words. "And when were you going to tell me this?"

He smiled and pulled her tighter. "As soon as you remembered that you are in love with me."

Beautiful happy tears streamed over her cheeks. He kissed each one.

"I'll never leave you, Lydia. I never did, you know. My heart was right here all along."

She nodded. "Oh, Joseph. Yours was here and mine was with you. I think they are better off together."

"Me, too."

"So, kiss me again, Joseph Yoder."

And he did. He kissed his Lydia softly and promised both her and God that he would kiss her every day in just this way and remember this moment when God brought them back together.

* * * * *

Dear Reader,

Thank you for reading *Return to Willow Trace*. I hope you enjoyed Joseph and Lydia's adventurous reunion. I thought it would be interesting to create a story with characters who had been in love with each other since childhood. As I wrote the story, I thought of these characters as I do of many admirable couples who meet early in life. I have always envied the thought of a soul mate as one's first love.

It was great fun working on this project and I am excited to have begun working on a new Amish suspense. Please join me for more Willow Trace stories and other tales of romantic suspense at www.kitwilkinson.com. Or write to me at write@kitwilkinson.com. I love to hear from readers.

Many Blessings,
Kit Wilkinson

Questions for Discussion

1. Joseph's character is a bit of a twist on the prodigal-son figure. Instead of leaving home to avoid responsibility and family duties, Joseph goes hoping to please his parents. Discuss the differences in the lessons of the prodigal-son story and those of Joseph. Which son suffers more?

2. Most of Lydia's struggles with Joseph are due to a lack of effective communication. If Joseph and Lydia were not Amish, thus using more modern and direct methods to be in touch with one another, would there still be issues between them? Why or why not?

3. Lydia is afraid to love because of her father's abandonment. Have you ever missed out on love or another opportunity because of fear? What was the regret, if any? Did you overcome this fear or do you still avoid certain situations?

4. "There is no fear in love. But perfect love drives out fear, because fear has to do with punishment" 1 John 4:18. How did Lydia punish herself? What do you think perfect love is? Is this something you give or get? Is it both? Do you think Lydia would have realized her fears without her mother's help?

5. Billy Ferris is both somewhat of a villain and a hero. After making so many bad choices in his

young life, he dies trying to reveal who Mr. Bowman really is. Discuss his role in the story. What events do you feel he is responsible for? What other things might have happened with or without Billy's role? In the end, do you find him to be more of a soft villain or more of a tragic hero?